# Hurricane S

## Robert Jackson

Copyright © Robert Jackson 1978

The right of Robert Jackson to be identified as the author of this work has been asserted by him in accordance with the Copyright, Designs and Patents Act, 1988.

First published in 1978 by Arthur Barker Limited.

This edition published in 2015 by Endeavour Press Ltd.

*The author wishes to thank Squadron Leader W. J. Rosser, DFC (RAF retired) and Lieutenant-Commander K. Calcutt (RN retired) for their invaluable help and advice.*

## Table of Contents

| | |
|---|---|
| CHAPTER ONE | 7 |
| CHAPTER TWO | 15 |
| CHAPTER THREE | 28 |
| CHAPTER FOUR | 37 |
| CHAPTER FIVE | 51 |
| CHAPTER SIX | 61 |
| CHAPTER SEVEN | 67 |
| CHAPTER EIGHT | 88 |
| CHAPTER NINE | 93 |
| CHAPTER TEN | 105 |
| CHAPTER ELEVEN | 116 |
| CHAPTER TWELVE | 128 |

# CHAPTER ONE

From ten thousand feet the River Somme looked for all the world like a basking snake, its coils shimmering in the early morning sun as they looped and twisted across the plain of Picardy west of Péronne. They lay six miles off the Hurricane's starboard wingtip, and in die narrow cockpit Sergeant George Yeoman allowed himself a small mental pat on the back; he was right on course.

He glanced down at the map on his knee, running his index finger along the thin pencil line of the track that ran from Manston, in Kent, to the little grass airstrip beside the Marne at Châlons: a distance of 179 miles. With a ground speed of 195 miles per hour, that gave him a flying time of fifty-five minutes. If all went well, he would be coming in to land at Châlons just before six o'clock, with plenty of time to make his report and stow his gear before breakfast.

Yeoman settled himself more comfortably in the cockpit, flexing his shoulders against the tight grip of the parachute harness. He was glad that he had decided to make an early start from Manston; it was a perfect morning, and navigation presented no difficulty despite the fact that the rising sun shone full in his eyes. Yeoman could not remember feeling happier. He was alone in the sky, with nothing but the roar of the big Rolls-Royce Merlin in front of him for company, on his way at last to join an operational squadron. For the next few minutes there was nothing to do but relax and enjoy the scenery — nothing, that was, except hold a steady course, check the landmarks as they came under the nose, and make an automatic scan of the instrument panel every now and then.

Idly, he wondered what his father would have made of the panorama that spread out on all sides. John Yeoman had taken his last look at the Somme four years before George had been born, and that had not been from a relatively comfortable seat two miles above the earth.

George would never know what his father had really been like before that terrible morning of 1 July 1916; all he knew was that its aftermath had dominated his childhood, remembering the anger and bitterness that had choked his father's voice whenever he had spoken of it. Now, looking down, it was almost impossible to imagine that nearly sixty thousand young men of George's own age, and many considerably younger, had been killed or wounded among those lovely wooded hillsides on that one morning alone, or that before the battle had ended in September 1916 the casualty lists had topped the half-million mark; a whole generation wiped out or scarred for life.

And now, twenty-four years later, the nations who had fought that deadly battle were once more at each other's throats; but there would never be another Somme. The tank and the dive-bomber had seen to that.

George remembered how deeply he had been moved by the stories of a friend, only a couple of years older than himself, who had come home, sallow-faced and trembling, in 1938 after a year in Spain with the International Brigade; stories of German dive-bombers, German fighters, German guns and German tanks, a whole army operating under the guise of volunteers and supported by an even larger contingent from Mussolini's Fascist Italy, mercilessly harrying the Republican forces to destruction.

The tragedy was that no one had seemed to care; or if they had cared, they had brushed their fears out of sight like dust under a rug. George's father had been one of them; he had dismissed the business of Czechoslovakia, and the rantings over the Sudetenland by Germany's Chancellor, Adolf Hitler, regarded by some as a genius and by others as a dangerous lunatic, as a gigantic bluff; he had been convinced that the Czech affair would blow over, even though the Germans had mobilized their army in August 1938 and had seemed ready to back up their words by force.

The illusions of John Yeoman, and millions of others like him, had been brutally shattered just a few weeks later, at the end of September. At Munich, with all pretence of a joint Anglo-French resistance to the demands of Nazi Germany thrown aside, Prime Ministers Neville Chamberlain of Britain and Daladier of France had capitulated to Hitler. The Allies would not go to the aid of Czechoslovakia if German forces invaded her; Germany could have the Sudetenland, with all its resources and frontier defences, and what matter if Czechoslovakia were stripped naked so long as the rest of Europe was saved from the spectre of war?

So Chamberlain had returned to London, brandishing the Munich agreement and proclaiming peace to a near-hysterical crowd; an uneasy, tenuous peace, little more than a breathing-space, bought by sacrificing the self-respect of Britain and France. And to John Yeoman, it had seemed that everything his friends had died for twenty years earlier had been wiped away by the stroke of a pen.

The straight, shining line of a canal came up ahead, cutting the Hurricane's track from north-east to southwest. The town over on the left was St Quentin; beyond it the canal curved away towards Cambrai, twenty miles to the north and falling behind in the distance.

St Quentin; Cambrai. Magic names in Yeoman's vocabulary. They were names that had captured the imagination of his youth when, in the long winter evenings, he had eagerly devoured books that had taken him into another world; a world of singing wind and humming wires, of roaring rotary engines and the drumming of fabric stretched taut over a wing; the world of Mannock, Immelmann, Ball and Richthofen, young men of a lost generation who had carved out a legend in the sky of Flanders, far above the mud in which his father had crawled.

George had wanted to fly for as long as he could remember. On leaving school he had got a job in a provincial newspaper office; it had hardly been inspiring work — his duties consisting mainly of fetching and carrying and making tea — but at least he had been able to put a bit of money aside towards his ultimate goal, which was getting into the air.

On his seventeenth birthday he had joined the nearest aero club, and after that he had lived only for weekends, cycling twenty miles for the privilege of half an hour in the draughty cockpit of a de Havilland Moth biplane. He had taken to the little machine readily and had gone solo quickly, after only three and a half hours' dual instruction, but it had been ten months before his logbook showed the total of nineteen hours that were necessary before he could take the test for his 'A' Licence. The flying test had been divided into two parts, an altitude test on the student's ability to lose height properly and make an accurate approach to land, and a 'figure of eights' test to prove that he was capable of making sustained and accurate steep turns. George had found difficulty with neither, and had passed the Royal Aero Club examiner's oral questions with a comfortable margin.

He smiled to himself, recollecting. It had all been worth it: the financial sacrifice, the long hours spent in a freezing cold hangar helping the mechanics when there was no flying. There had been times, of course, when he had wondered if he was doing the right thing; like the time he had applied to join the Auxiliary Air Force, armed with his brand-new flying licence, only to be turned down flat. The rejection, however, hadn't seemed so bad when someone had told him that the Auxiliaries were a toffee-nosed bunch of bastards anyway, and you didn't stand a chance of getting in unless you were in the habit of cavorting around the countryside after foxes.

Fortunately, the Royal Air Force Volunteer Reserve had not insisted on social attributes on the part of its applicants. The RAFVR, formed in 1936 to provide a nucleus of trained pilots, had accepted George readily and turned him into a Sergeant Pilot (Under Training) before he knew where he was, sending him and a bunch of others to a local civilian flying school for weekend training. Yeoman had started the course with the idea that he already knew a lot about flying, but his instructor — a quietly spoken man in his forties who had survived three years of the First World War flying observation aircraft over the enemy lines — had soon disillusioned him. George had been told in no uncertain terms that his civilian licence wasn't worth a damn, that he would have to start from scratch and that there was a lot more to military flying than performing nice-looking figures of eight. And, Yeoman had soon been forced to admit, his instructor had been right.

The year that followed had been the most hectic George had known so far. There had been no spare time; his job, and the demands of the VR — which insisted on his attending lectures on subjects such as navigation, theory of flight and armaments two evenings a week — had taken care of that. In the spring of 1939, after Hitler tore up the Munich Agreement and his Wehrmacht marched in to occupy the whole of Czechoslovakia, everything had assumed a new sense of urgency; the RAF was expanding rapidly and it was clear to most that the Service would soon need all the pilots it could get.

George and the friends he had made on the course had speculated a lot during that fateful summer, by which time they had left their faithful Tiger Moth primary trainers behind and were now flying more advanced Hawker Harts. They all felt that it was only a question of time before they received their mobilization orders. Things in Europe were moving fast now.

The orders had come at last on 28 August, three days before the Germans marched into Poland. The students had gone home to await orders, and on 3 September, together with millions of others, George had listened to the heavy, tired voice of Chamberlain, telling the world that everything he had striven towards was in ruins and that Great Britain, for the second time in a quarter of a century, was at war with Germany.

The next morning had found George on his way to Sealand, an airfield on the edge of the Dee Estuary in Flintshire. It was to be his home for the next ten weeks, and he had never worked harder. Sealand had resembled nothing closer than a huge sausage machine, devoted to teaching as many students as possible to fly Miles Master monoplanes — power-packed, speedy machines after the Tiger Moths and Harts George had been used to — within the available two months. Some, inevitably, fell by the wayside; George Yeoman was not among them. He had emerged in January 1940, continual bad weather having delayed the flying programme somewhat, with a total of 180 hours in his log-book and an unshakable feeling that he still had a great deal to learn.

The Hurricane trembled under him as he opened the throttle slightly, increasing the power; he was a couple of minutes behind on his ETA. He felt completely at home in the narrow confines of the cockpit, although it was less than two months since he had first got acquainted with the fighter. A lot had happened while he'd been going through Operational Training Unit; in April, the strange, unreal period of the Phoney War had been abruptly shattered when the Germans invaded Norway. At this very moment, he reflected, RAF fighter pilots were fighting what appeared to be a losing battle against a vastly superior enemy over the mountains and fjords. He envied them; they, at least, knew what it was like to shoot at Messerschmitts and Heinkels, instead of towed targets.

Still, he might soon have his chance. A few minutes ahead of him lay his first operational squadron, No. 505. The Hurricane he was flying was a brand-new machine, sent out to replace one lost in action. For, to the RAF's fighter pilots in France, the term 'Phoney War' had never had any real meaning.

Together with two other Hurricane squadrons and two equipped with the older Gloster Gladiator biplane fighters, No. 505 had been in France since the outbreak of war. Their task, in the main, would be to provide fighter cover for the ten squadrons of Fairey Battle light bombers that would be sent into action if the Germans attacked on the western front.

For months now, the RAF and French Air Force fighter squadrons had been skirmishing with the enemy over the Maginot Line, that great, supposedly impregnable structure stretching along the river Meuse. Some pilots had already made a name for themselves; one of them, a New Zealander named 'Cobber' Kain, had shot down a dozen or so enemy aircraft up to now, and a few others were climbing steadily up the ladder.

Yeoman suddenly remembered that it was Friday. He wondered if he would have the opportunity, over the weekend, to investigate the local countryside. He had a sudden nasty thought that it might be Friday the thirteenth, then grinned at the thought that he could hold any such foolish superstition. Anyway, it was the tenth. Friday, 10 May 1940. He was twenty years and one month old.

He glanced down, checking his map. For the last few minutes he had been flying over rolling, wooded hill country cut by a single wide river: the Aisne. Beyond the hills, ahead of him, lay a broad valley some ten miles across, bounded on the south by another spur of high ground; in the valley, easily identifiable ahead and to the left, at ten o'clock, was Reims.

He was fully alert now, his reverie pushed out of his mind by the business of getting the Hurricane down safely. He throttled back, beginning a gradual descent to three thousand feet. No point in trying to contact anyone over the R/T; his radio had died just after he had crossed the Channel, and there hadn't been a squeak out of it since.

The river Marne was under him now, with a tributary curving away northwards in the direction of Reims. A railway line crossed his track, running between Châlons-sur-Marne and Epernay, over on the right. He peered ahead, scanning the terrain to the south of Châlons, searching for the minute patch of open ground among the woods that would be the airfield. He spotted it without difficulty, nestling in the 'V' formed by the junction of two railway lines.

He reduced his speed to 140 miles per hour and joined overhead, looking down over the side of the cockpit, picking out a cluster of drab canvas tents. Nearby, eight or nine Hurricanes stood in a neat line, their camouflage making them difficult to spot against the sun-scorched grass.

Other aircraft, some familiar and some not — the latter presumably French types — were dotted here and there around the field.

A yellow windsock flapped limply, indicating a slight breeze from the west. He turned downwind, descending to a thousand feet and methodically carrying out his cockpit checks: undercarriage down, flaps down, fuel mixture fully rich, brakes off, propeller to fine pitch. A blast of air whirled into the cockpit as he reached up and opened the hood.

He brought the Hurricane down in a long, curving approach, with power on, turning towards the field into wind at five hundred feet and crossing the boundary at 86 miles per hour. The grass seemed to expand to meet him. He levelled the wings, easing back the stick and closing the throttle in a simultaneous movement. The fighter floated for a short distance, bounced slightly as the mainwheels touched, then the tail settled and she was firmly down, rumbling over the uneven ground.

He taxied forward, using short bursts of power, weaving from side to side to clear the blind area in front of the nose. Over by the parked Hurricanes an airman waited with raised arms, ready to marshal him into place.

Suddenly, Yeoman saw the man hurl himself to the ground. A split second later, the world blew up in his face.

There was a dim impression of a shadow, skipping over the cockpit. Then the ground ahead of him erupted in a great gout of smoke, earth and stones, accompanied by a terrific crash.

Instinctively, he threw an arm up in front of his face as the Hurricane slewed sideways, caught by the blast. The port undercarriage leg folded up and the wingtip struck the ground violently, tearing a long furrow. Yeoman was thrown forward brutally, banging his head on the gunsight.

Groggily, he clawed at his safety-harness release. Acrid smoke drifted into the cockpit, choking and blinding him; waves of hellish noise battered his ears.

Someone was pulling at his shoulders, helping him out of the cockpit. A voice was yelling something in his ear; he couldn't make any sense of the words. Then he was over the side, stumbling away from the crippled fighter, half supported by a figure who was still shouting at him. A shock wave hit him in the back like a giant hammer and the ground gave way under him. He was lying face down in a trench, with an enormous weight on top of him.

Suddenly his head cleared. He tried to sit up, spitting out soil. The weight was still on top of him. The words made sense now: 'For Christ's sake, keep your head down!' He cowered, trembling, in the bottom of the trench, as the earth shook beneath him.

Then, abruptly, it was over. The crash of explosions died away and the roar of engines faded in the distance, leaving only a strange crackling, roaring noise. The weight left him and he raised his head cautiously, peering over the edge of the trench. The crackling and roaring came from his Hurricane, which was blazing fiercely, sending dense smoke spiralling up into the morning air. A black pall was already forming over the field from other burning aircraft and bowsers. There were craters everywhere, like brown sores, and the air stank of cordite. A couple of the tents had disappeared, and he could see bodies scattered beside the wrecked flight line.

For the first time he turned to look at his companion, taking in the sergeant's stripes and the pilot's brevet, the green silk scarf wound loosely around the neck. Above the scarf a freckled, sunburned face grinned at him. The voice that addressed him had an unmistakable Texan drawl.

'That was a hell of an arrival. I guess the balloon's gone up at last. Sorry about your kite; we could have used her. By the way, I'm Jim Callender.'

Yeoman grasped the other's hand, still finding it hard to comprehend. Ten minutes earlier, he'd been enjoying the peace of a perfect morning; now he was crouching in a slit trench, covered with earth, being greeted by an American in RAF uniform. It was all too much. His head reeled and reaction knotted his stomach. He doubled over and was violently, uncontrollably sick.

# CHAPTER TWO

Fifty miles north-west of Châlons, at the junction of the river Oise and the St Quentin Canal, the awakening inhabitants of the little town of Chauny were not yet aware of the storm breaking in the east. The streets rang to the tune of metal-tipped clogs as the morning shift tramped to work in the chemical plant that was Chauny's life blood, now recovered and enriched after the devastation of 1914-18.

Only a few men realized the full gravity of the situation. In a rambling mansion on the outskirts of Chauny, to the accompaniment of the urgent, incessant shrilling of telephone bells, they pored over the maps that lay on a large oak table and gazed in stunned silence at the horrific picture that was slowly building up as report after report came in. The tension around the table was almost as visible as the smoke of pipes and pungent Gauloises, hanging in heavy blue wraiths in the beams of the morning sun.

Suddenly, there was an exclamation and one of the men slapped his open palm on the situation map with a crack that made everyone jump. Air Marshal Sir Arthur Barratt, commanding the British Air Forces in France, was finding it hard to control his temper.

He glared across the table at the man opposite, who wore the dark blue uniform of the *Armée de l'Air* — the French Air Force — and the gold braid of a general. This was d'Astier de la Vigerie, commander of France's northern zone of air operations. The contrast between the faces of the two men was remarkable. Barratt's showed open anger, while d'Astier's was creased by lines of anxiety and bewilderment. There was sadness there, too, born of the fact that he now found himself in a hopeless position and could do little to improve it.

Barratt raised his eyes from d'Astier, glancing briefly at the clock on the far wall. 'For God's sake,' he snapped, 'how much longer?'

It was ten-thirty, and for the past three hours Barratt — who was nominally under the orders of the French GHQ at Vincennes — had been vainly seeking authority to launch his squadrons of Battle and Blenheim bombers against the German armour and trucks that were jammed nose to tail on the narrow, winding tracks that ran through the Ardennes mountains. Now, he knew, was the time to strike, while the enemy concentrations were still vulnerable to air attack. Once the Panzers debouched from the mountains and began to spread out across the plains of Belgium and Luxembourg, the thinly scattered Allied bomber forces would be faced with a formidable task.

The trouble was that the French Commander-in-Chief, General Gamelin, and a lot of other senior officers too, were wary of releasing the Allied bombers in case the Luftwaffe took reprisals and started hammering France's towns and cities, in much the same way as they had done in Poland. Both Barratt and d'Astier knew this; they also knew that a golden opportunity to hit the enemy hard was slipping through their fingers with every passing minute.

While the French hesitated, the Germans acted. The situation reports told of airborne landings in Holland and Belgium, of dive-bomber attacks on frontier defences, of Allied aircraft burning on the ground before they had a chance to get into action. It seemed that the main enemy thrust was aimed at the point where the frontiers of Belgium, France and Luxembourg joined, and even now two armies — one French, the other British — were pushing forward as fast as they could to meet it. To the British and French commanders alike, it was becoming horribly clear that the Germans were staking everything on a bid to outflank the Maginot Line, that great and supposedly impregnable chain of armoured forts and minefields that stretched along France's eastern border from Switzerland to Belgium.

By eleven o'clock, Barratt could stand it no longer. Turning to the staff officers who had been sharing his frustration, he issued a series of rapid orders. Then, for the tenth time that morning, he had a telephone call put through to General Georges, the French military commander in the north.

Ten times, Georges — obeying the dictates of higher authority to the letter — had refused Barratt's request to send the bombers into action. This time, the Air Marshal did not seek approval. 'I intend,' he told Georges, 'to release my aircraft for offensive operations without further delay.'

Georges' defensive line was already beginning to crumble under the combined onslaught of Panzer and dive-bomber attacks. His attitude had changed dramatically since the last time Barratt spoke to him. He greeted the Air Marshal's initiative with just two words.

'Thank God!'

*

The surviving aircraft of 505 Squadron had flown two sorties since the whirlwind attack earlier that morning. The first patrol had been uneventful, and now the pilots who had stayed behind at Châlons for lack of serviceable aircraft — Yeoman and Callender among them — were lounging around the shack that served as an operations room, wandering outside from time to time to scan the eastern sky for a glimpse of the returning Hurricanes.

Yeoman had not yet had a chance to report to the CO, Squadron Leader Hillier. Events had moved too quickly for that, and there had been time only for a brief word with his flight commander, Flight-Lieutenant Rogerson, a small, balding man with a quiet voice whom Yeoman had liked instinctively from the first. Almost before the last echoes of the German attack had died away, Hillier had literally hurled himself into the air in pursuit of the enemy, followed by the other surviving Hurricanes in ones and twos. They had returned ninety minutes later, the pilots frustrated and cursing, to snatch a hasty mug of tea and a sandwich while sweating ground crews refuelled and rearmed the fighters for the second sortie.

Yeoman, still suffering slightly from his bang on the head and the furious pace of the morning, nevertheless felt a lot better for a breakfast of bacon sandwiches, washed down by scalding tea. Callender had taken advantage of their enforced inactivity to take him on a conducted tour and introduce him to some of their fellow NCOs. One of them, a dark, bull-necked flight sergeant armourer named Bert Duggan — who had spent most of the inter-war years in the Middle East and on India's North-West Frontier — left Yeoman with few illusions about the Air Striking Force's state of readiness.

'Bloody stuff's useless,' he grunted, aiming a contemptuous kick at a crate of .303 ammunition. 'It's been in store since about 1918. Bloody wogs up the Khyber had a better chance of shooting something down than you blokes have. Take my advice; you get a Jerry up your backside, stick your nose down and run like hell.'

Callender called Duggan a miserable old bastard and laughed off the remark. Later, however, he confided to Yeoman that there was a lot of truth behind the Flight Sergeant's pessimism.

'Don't get him wrong — he really is a first-rate sort, and he knows what he's talking about. He was an air gunner himself once, on the frontier. He once flew a Wapiti back to base when his pilot was wounded, but he pranged on landing and the guy up front got killed. He was knocked about a bit, that's why he walks with a limp. Got recommended for a gong, but the paperwork got screwed up in the system somewhere.' Callender lit a cigarette and went on thoughtfully: 'Seriously, it's a bit of a bloody shambles out here. I remember when we first arrived, the Frogs were supposed to have laid everything on for us, but in fact we were grounded for the best part of a week because there was no fuel. Getting hold of spares is murder, too. We've no storage facility here, and everything we want has to be hauled over from Cherbourg. We're only fifty per cent serviceable, most of the time.'

Yeoman nodded towards the operations room wall, on which hung an aluminium plate bearing a Luftwaffe unit insignia and the legend '2/Aufklr.Gr.33'. It had been taken from one of the squadron's victories, a Dornier 17 reconnaissance aircraft. 'But you still manage to knock down Jerries,' he commented.

'Right,' Callender replied, 'but only when we happen to be in the right place at the right time. They come in high and fast, and even when we have the height advantage we have a hell of a job catching them. The French have a warning system of sorts, which is supposed to give us time to get airborne, but it's hopeless. It depends on land-lines, and if you've ever tried to make a phone call in France you'll know what I'm talking about. Believe it or not, all their military calls go through civilian exchanges. By the time we get the word, Jerry's recce boys have been and gone.'

The spitting crackle of a Merlin engine being started interrupted the conversation briefly. Callender grinned. 'Well, that's one they've got going. Chiefy Thomas — you haven't met him yet, but if you come across a guy that looks like Tarzan's sidekick, with a mouthful of spark plugs, that's him — said they'd have three serviceable by eleven-thirty, and he hasn't let us down yet.'

Yeoman sensed that Callender was trying to change the subject, but he was in no mood to let his new friend off the hook. He was learning a lot, and none of it agreed with what he had been told back home. 'What about the Messerschmitts?' he asked.

Callender looked at him and raised an eyebrow. 'Ah yes, now there's a thing. You want me to sum them up, is that it? All right. They're small, they're nimble, they're faster than us, they have a better rate of climb than us, a better ceiling than us, they have two machine-guns and a bloody great cannon that fires through the spinner, they hang around over the Maginot Line in swarms, their tactics are bloody superb and they shoot down our recce aircraft like flies. Does that answer your question?'

Yeoman was silent. He gazed at Callender, willing him to go on.

'Look,' Callender continued, 'let me explain. Some of those Jerry fighter leaders have got four years of action behind them, first in Spain and then in Poland. They don't muck about with tight, parade-ground battle formations, like us, where you have to work so bloody hard to keep up with the guy next to you that you never have time to see who else is in your bit of sky; they fly loose, in twos and fours, like this.' He grabbed a pencil and paper and drew a quick sketch for Yeoman's benefit.

'You can see,' he went on, 'that their battle formations are organized so that collectively the pilots can scan the sky all around. Their basic formation is a pair, with the leader shooting down aircraft and his number two protecting his tail.'

'That's not new,' Yeoman commented, recalling the books he had read as a boy. 'Boelcke used the same tactics in 1916. So why don't we use them too?'

Callender shrugged. 'Good question. Plenty of our blokes have pushed the idea, and a lot of them would still be alive if it had been taken up. Rogerson tried it off his own bat with "B" Flight a few weeks ago, and got an almighty bollocking from Hillier for his pains. Hillier's a good pilot — they reckon his solo aerobatics used to steal the show at Hendon before the war — but he insists on doing everything by the book. Probably fornicates by numbers, I shouldn't wonder.'

Yeoman was lost in thought. If what Callender said was true, it made nonsense of the tactics that had been drummed into the newcomer at the operational training unit. For the first time, he felt something close to panic at the thought of going into action. He felt lost and helpless in the face of the other's experience. 'So what the blazes do we do?' he asked.

Callender grinned. 'That's easy. If you get one of those sons of bitches on your tail, you turn and keep on turning. It's the one thing the Hurricane can do better than the 109 can do. The Messerschmitt has a high wing-loading, and it tends to stall out of a tight turn. When that happens, you've got him. If he tries to hit you at speed from higher up, turn to meet him. Nine times out of ten, he'll break off to the right at the last moment — and in that case, too, you've got him.'

Yeoman, eager for more information, was on the point of asking further questions when the drone of distant aero-engines interrupted him. Both men went to the door and shaded their eyes against the sun. A couple of miles away, high up, a flight of three monoplanes skimmed below a line of fleecy cloud, heading south-east.

'Hurricanes?' ventured Yeoman. Callender shook his head. 'They're French. Morane 406s. Those guys really have a rough time of it; the Morane's no match for the 109.'

'What are the French like — in action, I mean?' Yeoman wanted to know.

'They're good fighters, and they have plenty of guts. But their organization is hopeless, and so is most of their equipment. Their best fighter is American, the Curtiss Hawk, and the groups using it have notched up some pretty good scores over the Saar — but there just aren't enough of them. They don't have much freedom of action, either; their main purpose in life seems to be escorting recce aircraft. Jerry usually waits until they are well inside his own territory, then hits them hard and fast from upstairs. The 109s don't always come out on top, but they usually manage to clobber the recce kite.'

Callender lit another cigarette from the butt of the previous one. 'I admire those recce crews, poor bastards,' he continued. 'Our lot gave up committing that kind of suicide months ago. In the early days, last September, they used to send formations of Battles over the front line in daylight until the 109s knocked down four out of five one day. The Blenheims didn't do much better, either; fifty per cent casualties isn't anybody's idea of good arithmetic, and the upshot of it all is that we really haven't a clue about what's been happening on the other side.' He threw his freshly lit cigarette down and ground it contemptuously into the floor with his heel. 'No wonder the sods caught us with our knickers down.'

There was a sudden yell of derision and a copy of *Punch* sailed across the room and hit Callender in the back of the neck. A man got up from a basket chair in the comer and strolled over, grinning. Yeoman, who had only half-noticed him before, now saw that he was a flight sergeant pilot, with the ribbon of the Distinguished Flying Medal under his brevet. He had jet-black hair and an impressive handlebar moustache, and two of his top front teeth were missing.

'Allow me to introduce myself,' said the newcomer, 'since this ignorant refugee from Gettysburg obviously has no intention of doing so. My name is Simon Wynne-Williams, and I might add —' glaring with mock ferocity at Callender — 'that one of my distinguished ancestors fought against these wretched colonials at Bunker Hill. He got killed, but that's beside the point. I am convinced,' he went on darkly, 'that this fellow was deliberately infiltrated into our gallant ranks with the object of spreading alarm and despondency among our excellent young pilots, who may be picked out from the general herd by the fact that their eyes fill with spaniel-like adoration when they gaze upon elderly and much-decorated veterans, such as myself.'

Yeoman laughed, sensing that there was real friendship between these two. 'Come to think of it,' he asked Callender, 'how does a Yank like you come to be mixed up in somebody else's war?'

Callender feigned indignation. 'Cheeky young cub, calling your elders and betters names! I'll have you know I was flying aeroplanes when you were still wiping your snotty nose on your sleeve, and it stands to reason that the Air Force should snap up pilots of such brilliance.'

Wynne-Williams grinned. 'Actually, he's only a pretend American. His old man might own a railroad in Texas, but his mother's as English as you are, and ...' His words were cut off by the harsh clamour of the telephone on the ops-room desk. A bored-looking corporal, who had been sitting next to it reading a comic, looked at the instrument as though it were about to explode, then picked it up cautiously and muttered into it. A moment later, he clapped a hand over the mouthpiece and addressed Wynne-Williams. 'Flight, it's a wingco from Panther. (HQ Advanced Air Striking Force.) He wants to speak to who-ever's in charge.'

Wynne-Williams looked around as though seeking an avenue of escape, but he was the most senior man in the room. All the officers were airborne. He took the phone and held a clipped conversation with the man on the other end of the line. The others listened intently, trying to make sense of the snatches they heard. Wynne-Williams scribbled information on a scrap of paper as he talked. 'Right, sir ... I think we should have three in fifteen minutes ... pick them up at twelve-fifteen, on the way out ... what about authorization? Fine ... We'll do our best.'

He replaced the receiver and turned to look at Callender and Yeoman, allowing a low whistle of air to escape through the gap in his teeth. 'Well, gentlemen,' he said, 'this looks like our chance to be heroes. I've just been informed that thirty-odd Battles are on their way to attack enemy columns advancing through Luxembourg. Panther's trying to rake up some fighter cover, and apparently not doing very well. Everybody's either airborne or in a state of complete chaos.'

He paused and looked hard at Callender. 'What it amounts to,' he went on, 'is a direct order to get off the ground with whatever we have left and give those poor bastards a hand. The wingco I just talked to says he'll take the responsibility, but you know what Hillier's like — if we go off without proper authorization he'll probably nail us to the flagpost by our balls. Still, I'm game to stick my neck out. What about you?'

The American nodded. 'Sure,' he said softly, 'why not?' Yeoman rose eagerly from his chair. 'Me too.' His stomach was turning over with excitement and a tinge of fear.

'Right,' Wynne-Williams yelled, 'what are we standing here gassing for? Let's get on with it!'

Fifteen minutes later they were airborne, the ground crews — driven like slaves by Flight Sergeant Thomas — having broken all records to get three Hurricanes into some state of airworthiness. They climbed steadily away from Châlons in a tight 'V' formation, turning on to a heading of 050 degrees for Luxembourg. Wynne-Williams was leading, with Callender flying in the number two position and Yeoman in number three.

The engine of Yeoman's aircraft was running roughly and he had some difficulty in keeping station behind and to the left of Wynne-Williams. He played with the throttle, trying to find the best setting, and was relieved when the vibration stopped and the roar of the Merlin steadied.

They climbed to eight thousand feet, still holding a north-easterly heading. They crossed the broad, swift-flowing Meuse to the north of Verdun, that everlasting symbol of France's gallantry and sacrifice in a bygone war, and Wynne-Williams's voice came over the radio, crackling and distorted: 'All right, spread out and keep your eyes peeled. George, watch out for the Battles, they'll be low and ahead of us. Jim, watch that cloud cover to starboard.'

Yeoman realized with a sudden shock that this was his first operational flight. He had only a confused idea of what he might have expected, but it wasn't this — not an aircraft to be seen apart from the Hurricanes, no swarms of Messerschmitts, no flames of war, nothing except the rolling, wooded foothills of the Ardennes, intersected by glittering rivers.

They flew on for ten more minutes. The city of Luxembourg, nestling like a spider in its web of converging roads and railways, was ahead and to the right, six or seven miles away. On the far horizon, the pilots could now see a cluster of what looked like slender black fingers, pointing skywards and joining at the top in a flat, indistinct layer. They were columns of smoke. Over there, beneath them, men were fighting and dying.

There was still no sign of the returning Battles. Yeoman, who had been straining his eyes in his search for the bombers — which would be hard to spot against the greens and browns of the terrain — looked up and blinked sharply as what seemed to be a shaft of mirrored sunlight struck his retina. A few moments later he saw it again, and this time knew it for what it was: the glitter of an aircraft's wing.

His hand moved towards the R/T transmitter switch, but Wynne-Williams had seen the aircraft too and it was his warning that came crackling first over the air. On his orders the three Hurricanes began a climbing turn to port, towards the other machines.

They were clearly visible now, half a dozen silvery crosses skimming through the tufts of cumulus like a shoal of fish. They were heading west, and the Hurricanes had the sun behind them as they climbed.

Yeoman switched on his reflector sight, checking range and wingspan indicators. The note of the Merlin altered slightly as he adjusted the propeller pitch. A quick scan of the instruments told him that the oil temperature was a little on the high side, but apart from that everything seemed all right. He moved the gun-button to 'fire'.

The Hurricanes climbed flat out in line abreast, the pilots' eyes glued on the other aircraft. Yeoman's stomach lurched and a hot wave of mingled fear and excitement swept over him as he made positive identification. Short, square-cut wings, tail-planes set high on the fins, slender, shark-like fuselages — there was no mistaking the angular outlines of the Messerschmitt 109.

The 109s were flying in pairs, well spaced out and in echelon to starboard. They seemed to be in no hurry, and the hard-climbing British fighters had little trouble in overhauling them. They were a couple of thousand feet above the enemy now, still in line abreast, curving to the attack with the sun behind them. The German formation cruised on steadily, seemingly oblivious to the danger.

Wynne-Williams's voice was as calm as if he were taking part in a training flight. 'All right, spread out. We'll attack in line abreast. I'll take the centre pair. George, you take the two on the left. No heroics. One pass, then get the hell out of it. Get stuck in!'

A strange feeling descended on Yeoman as he opened the throttle. His heart pounded, yet he felt no fear. All that mattered was the target in front of him. The details stood out clearly now; the blotchy grey camouflage, the stark black crosses. Out of the corner of his eye he saw the other two Hurricanes, matching him in the dive.

The Messerschmitt on the extreme left hung squarely in his sight. Two hundred yards ... a hundred and fifty. Get in close, like they did in the old days. Sweat was pouring into his eyes. Never mind, to hell with it.

One hundred yards. Now! His thumb punched the firing-button. The Hurricane shuddered frighteningly. Grey smoke trails streamed towards the Messerschmitt. Everything was suspended in slow motion. The grey trails arrowed past the enemy's port wing. Christ, missed! Right rudder, fire again on the skid. The Messerschmitt broke hard, to the left, and the smoky lines disappeared into the fuselage behind the cockpit.

A sudden puff of smoke. A sheet of metal, tearing away and whirling back, barely missing Yeoman's cockpit. Close. Christ, too close! He was going to hit the 109. He was going to die. A moment of blind panic. A great black shadow, gone in an instant, as the 109, on its back now, flashed over the Hurricane with feet to spare.

In that instant, braced in the cockpit to meet the awful impact that never came, his head flung back, Yeoman saw the face of his enemy.

Like a single frame from a movie film it flickered before him and vanished. The face of a man, white beneath a black helmet, mouth gaping in fear and, perhaps, pain.

A glance back. The 109 spinning, staining the sky with a question-mark of smoke. Something moving into his field of vision, astern and from the right. Swivel the head the other way, fast. Oh God, another 109 almost on his tail, firing already in short bursts, tracers flickering past. Turn. Turn. Fight away the fear that comes back to turn your guts to water and keep turning. The Hurricane can out-turn a 109. You know it can, so keep turning, tighter all the time. Forget about everything except the pressure on the rudder and the stick in your stomach, keeping the glittering disc of the propeller on the horizon. Tighten the turn even further, wings almost perpendicular, the brute force of it pushing your backside into the seat A glance in the mirror. The 109 still there, but off to the right, trying and failing to turn inside you. More tracer, falling away towards the patchwork fields far below.

The Hurricane shuddered, battered by a series of staccato bangs. Oil sprayed back, smothering the windscreen with a black film. The roar of the tortured Merlin stopped abruptly and the fighter's nose dropped as she fell out of the turn, flicking into a spin.

In that split second, Yeoman knew he had not been hit. It was the engine. The bloody engine. A glance at the altimeter: ten thousand feet. Let her spin; it was his only chance now of shaking off the bastard on his tail. Let the German think he'd bought it.

Eight thousand feet. Dust and bits of paper whirled around the cockpit. The earth gyrated in a crazy blur in front of his eyes. Check everything. Fuel. Mixture. Throttle. Get ready. No time to look back, just concentrate on spin recovery.

Five thousand feet. Now for it. Full opposite rudder, ease the pressure off the stick a little to unstall the wings. The Hurricane went on spinning, with no apparent slowing of the rate of rotation. An illusion. Give her time. Hold on full rudder.

The ground beneath him slowed and then stood still. Gently, he pulled back the stick, nursing the fighter out of its dive, taking care not to make his control movements too abrupt. With a dead engine, it would be all too easy to enter another spin — and if that happened, with the altimeter now showing less than three thousand feet, the odds were that he would come out of it at about the same time as he hit the ground.

He flattened out, trimming the Hurricane for the glide, looking over his shoulder as he did so. There was no sign of the Messerschmitt. His main problem now was to get his aircraft down in one piece. It would not be easy; the terrain that crawled underneath him was hilly and wooded. He briefly considered the possibility of baling out, then rejected it. He was too low.

He turned downwind to stretch his glide a little, frantically searching ahead for somewhere to land. A few hundred yards off to the left, a hillside sloped down towards a river. It seemed to be relatively clear of trees and other obstacles and he turned towards it. He would use his last few hundred feet of height to gain some speed, then flatten out and land up the slope. It would be tricky and dangerous, but there was no alternative.

Everything was still switched on. He reached for the fuel cock, but his hand never touched it.

Suddenly, miraculously, the Hurricane's propeller kicked over a couple of times. Instinctively, Yeoman seized the throttle lever and pumped it. The propeller turned a few more times, gratingly, sending shivers through the airframe. Then the Merlin picked up with a coughing roar and the propeller blades dissolved in a blur. It was the most beautiful sight Yeoman had ever seen.

The ground was dangerously close. Trees were drifting up to meet him and he opened the throttle wide in a fluid movement, resisting the temptation to slam it open. Slowly, painfully, the Hurricane began to climb. Not fast enough. A line of trees at the top of the slope filled his vision.

He reached down and jerked the flap lever. The flaps came down with a thump and the fighter bounded fifty feet into the air as the precious extra lift took effect. One hand held the throttle hard against the stop, the other pulled back the stick. Yeoman shut his eyes in an instinctive reflex as the treetops sped to meet him, then forced them open again. There was nothing but clear sky in his windscreen. He looked round. Part of a tree branch trailed from his starboard wingtip. He hadn't felt the jolt.

He climbed away, trying to work out where he was. He was finding the Hurricane hard to control, and realized with a sudden shock that the trembling of his hands was to blame. He became conscious of acute physical discomfort His arms and legs ached from the strain of throwing the Hurricane around the sky; he could feel sweat trickling down the inside of his legs, turning his socks into sodden pulp. He was very thirsty, and his eyes felt raw.

He took the Hurricane up to six thousand feet and settled down on a heading of 260 degrees. He had little trouble in picking up landmarks, and landed at Châlons fifteen minutes later.

As he taxied in, another Hurricane touched down. He looked for the code letters; it was Jim Callender's aircraft, its rear fuselage in shreds where enemy bullets had tom it.

Wynne-Williams was missing. Callender had seen him go down into a wood. There had been no parachute.

# CHAPTER THREE

Joachim Richter sat on the edge of his bed and stared moodily at the framed document on the wall. It read: 'In the Name of the Führer! I appoint Senior Flight Cadet Joachim Richter to the rank of Lieutenant, effective 30 March 1940.

'I confirm this appointment in full expectation that through conscientious performance of his duty as an officer in accordance with his oath of service and loyalty, the confidence shown by the award of this Commission to the above-named will be justified. He on his part may call upon the special protection of the Führer.

'Dated at Berlin, this 15th Day of April 1940. Signed: Goering, Reich Minister for Aviation and Commander-in-Chief of the Air Force.'

It had been his proudest possession. He had worked hard for it ever since the day, eighteen months earlier, when he had reported as a raw recruit to the basic flying school at Schönewalde.

Any illusion that he was going to jump straight into an aircraft's cockpit had been quickly swept aside. Life over the next four months had been one hard slog, alternating between the parade ground and the lecture room. The drill sessions had been a nightmare: especially the obligatory parade marches, the ceremonial 'goose-stepping' that had transformed leg muscles into searing knots of agony and toes into bruised, bloody pulp. He had hated the drill instructors; brutal, bullying men who screamed, never speaking in normal tones. The hatred had seen him through. They hadn't made him as tough as Krupp's steel — their favourite expression — but they had nurtured in him a deep determination never to be beaten. Perhaps, on reflection, that was what their job was all about.

The lecture periods had come as a tremendous relief, a time of leisure almost, when he had been able to submerge himself in the mysteries of aerodynamics and navigation. Then had come the day of his first flying lesson, in a Focke-Wulf FW 44 biplane, and suddenly all the square-bashing, all the crawling through mud in full field kit, had seemed worthwhile.

He had sailed through his primary flying course, gaining his pilot's certificate just after the outbreak of war. Two weeks later, exalting in the rank of corporal, he had reported for operational training at a fighter school. He counted himself exceptionally lucky; most of his friends had been posted to dive-bombers.

His first fighter type had been something of a disappointment. It was a high-wing Arado Ar 68 monoplane, a mid-1930s aircraft which the Luftwaffe used for fighter conversion. All in all, it wasn't a great deal different from the Focke-Wulfs and Gothas he had been used to. Top speed was a hard-earned 195 miles per hour, and the machine's low-speed handling characteristics were appalling.

After the Ar 68, he had graduated on to the Messerschmitt 109 — and that was altogether a different kettle of fish. He was not unduly tall, but he had found the 109's cockpit cramped and claustrophobic until he got used to it. The little beast's handling left no room for error, either, especially on landing. The approach speed had to be just right, or else you either overshot hopelessly or spun in and killed yourself. A few of his friends had ended their careers abruptly that way.

By the time he left fighter school he had fallen in love with the 109, despite her vices. She was like a temperamental woman, terribly unforgiving of any rough treatment. Caress her, and she wouldn't let you down. Maltreat her, and she would kick back hard.

He couldn't remember a better time than those weeks at fighter school. The airfield had been only a few miles from Berlin, so there had been plenty of distractions to fill his off-duty hours and compensate for the intensive training programme. The capital had been teeming with night-life and gaiety; the German people, even those who covertly doubted the wisdom of Hitler's war, were riding high on a wave of optimism. A uniform, especially a Luftwaffe uniform, had attracted the girls like a magnet.

His posting to Fighter Wing 66, just in time to take part in the opening phase of Plan Yellow — the attack in the west — had been the fulfilment of a dream. Formed on the Western Front in 1917, the wing had carved out a reputation second only to Richthofen's unit. It had been reformed in 1934, and the pilots who now led it had fought in both the Spanish Civil War and Poland. It was an honour to be assigned to it; an honour that fell, as everyone knew, to only the most promising of Goering's 'young eagles'.

The wing had moved up to Bitburg on 8 May, and had been held in reserve during the dawn air strikes forty-eight hours later. It was not until noon that Richter had taken off on his first operational sortie — an offensive patrol over Luxembourg.

He slammed his fist hard against the bed-rail as a mixture of black fury and self-pity overwhelmed him. His first combat trip — and he had made an unholy mess of it. Splashed a great black blot over his copybook that would take months to eradicate. And it hadn't been all his fault; that was the worst of it. But no matter whose fault it had been, nothing was going to bring back Schindler, Klaus and Reinecke.

A tap on the door brought him back to his immediate surroundings. He stood up, reluctantly, to face the man who entered.

The newcomer wore the insignia of a captain and decorations that betokened active service in Spain and Poland. He was a small man, with a rather ugly face and black hair, brushed straight back and parted in the middle. His smile, however, was friendly, and Richter took an instinctive liking to him. The man was a stranger; probably one of the pilots of Fighter Wing 53, a detachment of which had arrived at Bitburg that morning.

The man made no move to introduce himself. Instead, he strolled casually across the room and draped himself over an armchair. He looked at Richter and raised an eyebrow.

'I hear you had a spot of bother,' he said. Richter sat down on the bed again and nodded miserably.

'Want to talk about it?'

The young pilot sighed. Maybe it would do him good to get the whole thing off his chest. He lit a cigarette, drew on it heavily, then looked at it distastefully and crushed it out.

'Tastes like sawdust,' he muttered. 'It's a pipe for me from now on.' He ran his hand through his hair and began to tell his story, hesitantly at first, then with more confidence as the man in the armchair nodded encouragement.

'We were patrolling over Luxembourg at four thousand metres — a flight of six. I was flying wingman in number two section. Anyway, we got hit by three Hurricanes. The Tommies came right down out of the bit of sky I was supposed to be watching. I never even saw them. The first I knew about it was when my number one blew up. One second he was there — the next there was nothing but a cloud of smoke with bits falling out of it.

'I didn't see the Tommy who got him. I broke hard left and swung under the rest of the formation, just in time to see another Tommy hit Reinecke in number three section. I got on the Hurricane's tail and we turned round one another for a few minutes. I managed to get in a few bursts, but I don't know whether I hit him or not. I might have done, because he suddenly flicked into a spin. I don't know what happened to him. I had my work cut out with another Hurricane, but he skipped off after a while.'

The stranger scratched his nose. 'So what's your problem?' he asked.

'The problem,' Richter replied, 'is that I'm being held responsible for what happened. We lost three pilots, and I'm to blame. I didn't keep a good lookout.'

He shuddered inwardly, recalling what had happened after he had landed. His squadron commander, Major Hartwig, had assembled all his pilots together in the ante-room of the mess and then forced Richter to stand on a table in the middle. All right, so one of the dead pilots — Reinecke — had been Hartwig's closest friend, but that had not justified the humiliation to which he, Richter, had been subjected. His ears still burned from the dressing-down Hartwig had given him, in front of the embarrassed assembly. He had stood there, miserable and red-faced, as close to tears as he had been since he was a child, for what seemed an eternity before Hartwig had allowed him to flee to the sanctuary of his room.

The stranger rose from the armchair and strolled across the room, standing in front of the window with his hands behind his back. He turned and surveyed Richter thoughtfully.

'First operation?' he asked. Richter nodded.

The other grinned. 'All right. So we all make mistakes. Look at the fellows m the last war. Immelmann, for instance. Wrecked more aircraft than you've had hot dinners before he even got his pilot's licence. I know your problem — you wanted to make a great impression, right from the start, and you think you've let everyone down — worst of all, that you've let yourself down.'

He wagged a finger at Richter. 'I'm sorry about the three fellows who didn't come back, but this is war and such things happen. I don't intend to condemn your squadron commander, either. He was quite right to give you a bollocking. It will help the others to learn from your mistake and probably save some of their lives, one day. But console yourself with this thought: there were more pairs of eyes than yours in that formation, and they didn't see any danger either.'

He moved towards the door. 'What you need right now,' he went on, 'is a strong coffee or two and a long talk about tactics. All this will be forgotten tomorrow. This war is going to last for a long time, never mind what anyone says. There'll be plenty more Tommies for you to have a crack at.'

Richter got up, straightening his tunic. Already, he felt as though a black cloud had been lifted from his mind. He felt that he owed a great debt to this man, and said so. Then, almost as an afterthought, he asked the other's name.

The stranger turned, clicking his heels and giving a small, almost mocking bow, extending his hand at the same time.

'Mölders,' he said. 'Werner Mölders.'

\*

Had Richter but known it, the 'Tommy' with whom he had been locked in mortal combat a bare two hours earlier was having every bit as hard a time, and the German might have derived some small consolation from the fact.

Yeoman was at that moment standing rigidly to attention in front of the trestle table that served as his commanding officer's desk, with Callender in the same posture beside him. Yeoman kept his eyes fixed firmly on the map on the opposite wall; anything was better than meeting Hillier's stony gaze.

Squadron Leader Richard Fitzhugh Hillier was an angry man. He was also weary, and nursing an inward misery that he dare not show. He had lost three pilots that morning — four, counting Wynne-Williams — and that was far from good arithmetic in exchange for six enemy aircraft destroyed.

He held a pencil between the tips of his index fingers and rotated it slowly, switching his gaze coldly from Yeoman to Callender and back again.

'You are a pair of bloody fools.' His voice was low and even, but it cut like a whiplash. 'Let me just catalogue your stupidity. First of all, you take off on a so-called escort sortie. An unauthorized escort sortie into the bargain.' He threw the pencil on to the table. It rolled across the top and clattered on the floor.

'Christ!' Hillier exploded, rising abruptly and planting both palms flat on the table, leaning forward to glare at the two pilots. 'Somebody rings up and says he's a wing commander on the Panther staff, and on the strength of that you launch yourselves off on some wild goose chase! Did you find the Battles? Did you hell! Instead, you decide to take on a Jerry formation and be heroes. I don't care if you do claim to have knocked a couple down — the fact remains that one of you didn't come back and that both your aircraft are knackered. That leaves me with five serviceable aircraft to fight half the blasted Luftwaffe. What happens now if the bomber boys really need our help? Stupid pair of bastards!'

He sat down again and sighed heavily, passing a hand over his face. His voice became suddenly weary. 'I need pilots,' he said. 'You can thank God for that. Otherwise I'd bust you so low you'd be able to crawl under a door. Just remember this: I will not tolerate individual heroics. This squadron is a team and it's going to stay that way. Now get out.'

The two saluted, turned on their heels and marched out. Hillier lit a cigarette and stared moodily at the map on the wall. He hated tearing strips off his men, but survival was what counted now and if they were going to survive they would have to pull together. Callender was a good pilot, but wild; he'd have to watch that. Young Yeoman had shown up well, taking everything into account. He'd be all right — if he lived long enough.

Hillier wondered how the other AASF fighter squadrons were getting on. No one seemed to know what was happening, except that a lot of airfields had been bombed and the Luftwaffe was everywhere. There were a lot of rumours flying about, but Hillier discounted most of them. According to the grapevine, the countryside was stiff with enemy agents and parachutists, all of them disguised as priests and nuns. Hillier had a pretty good idea that the rumours had been started deliberately in order to spread panic, and he proposed to take no chances. He had already ordered the airfield perimeter guard to be doubled, and had instructed his pilots to carry sidearms at all times.

The telephone shrilled. It was Panther, requesting a standing patrol over the Air Headquarters at Reims. Bastards, he thought, sitting nice and secure in their concrete champagne cellars. They were probably burning their paperwork already. He grabbed his flying helmet and stamped out, slamming the door behind him.

\*

Yeoman lay stretched out under a tree, his head resting on a parachute pack. Callender sat beside him, idly flicking at the May bugs which were dropping from the branches like miniature paratroops. The heat was stifling, and the shade afforded scant relief. Yeoman couldn't remember a time when he had felt so dirty. His body was caked with sweat and grime and he longed for a bath. His head ached intolerably, his eyes hurt and his throat felt as though coarse sandpaper had been passed over it.

A section of Hurricanes roared off, momentarily drowning the rumble of bombing in the distance. Yeoman watched as they swung away to the northwest, in the direction of Reims. He felt thoroughly miserable. He didn't give a damn if he never sat in an aircraft's cockpit again. Everything and everyone seemed to be against him, including the intelligence officer. Yeoman had put in a claim for a 109 destroyed, but since he had not seen the aircraft crash or the pilot bail out, the intelligence officer had only awarded him 'one damaged' — and grudgingly at that.

He jumped as a clod of earth hit him on the chest. He looked up to see Callender grinning at him. 'Come on, snap out of it. You look like a centipede with corns.'

Yeoman shrugged. 'Just feel cheesed off, that's all.'

Callender's face became serious. 'If my guess is correct you soon won't have time to feel cheesed off. None of us will.' He waved a hand in the general direction of the muted bombing. 'Listen to that. Somebody's getting plastered, and it'll be our turn again before long. We've already lost more than half our kites, and we haven't even had a chance to get stuck in yet. Much more of this, and we'll be fighting with balloons on sticks.'

Bert Duggan came over, his bull neck even redder than usual, and filled a fire bucket from a small water bowser that was standing nearby. He buried his nose in the bucket and drank thirstily, then tipped the rest of the water over his head. He shook himself like a dog, grunted at Yeoman and Callender, then shambled off.

'There goes one hell of a fine guy,' Callender said softly. 'He'll be working his men like slaves, but you can bet your last dollar he'll be working twice as hard himself. It's people like —'

Callender broke off abruptly and scrambled up, his eyes on the armourer. Duggan had stopped and was staring at the eastern sky, his head making small jerky movements like a dog scenting a quarry. Suddenly he turned and began to run towards the operations shack, waving his arms and shouting something to the small group of pilots who lounged on the grass outside. Yeoman and Callender, who were fifty yards away, couldn't make out what Duggan was saying.

Callender looked at the sky. An aircraft was making its approach to land, but it was only a Fairey Battle. There was no apparent danger, and Callender turned to Yeoman with a puzzled expression on his face. He opened his mouth to speak, then froze as his companion jumped up, his arm outflung and pointing.

Beyond the Battle, flying very low and very fast, skimming the hedgerows, three twin-engined aircraft were bearing down on the airfield. The Battle crew must have seen them too, because the aircraft suddenly dived steeply as the pilot tried to lose height in a desperate attempt to get down before the enemy caught up with him.

He was too late. The leading aircraft — identifiable now as a Messerschmitt 110 — opened fire, raking the luckless Battle almost casually as it swept past. The light bomber, its undercarriage down, hit the ground and bounced, shedding fragments. The wheels folded up as it struck the ground again, sliding on its belly for a hundred yards before slewing to a stop.

Yeoman and Callender hurled themselves flat under their tree as the Messerschmitts howled over the field. Horrified, Yeoman saw two airmen, running for their lives, blown apart by cannon shells. The Messerschmitts broke to left and right and turned, running in from the opposite direction. A pile of fuel drums exploded with a dull boom, turning a screaming airman into a torch.

Yeoman raised his head, then buried it under his arms again as shells and bullets raised fountains of earth a few yards in front of his eyes. The trail of fire swept towards the operations shack and punched holes in it, filling the interior with a hornet's nest of splinters which, miraculously, left the duty corporal unscathed.

The snarl of engines died away. Belatedly, the antiaircraft guns around the airfield perimeter began to bark, their shells spraying the countryside with shrapnel and doing no damage at all to the attackers.

Yeoman and Callender scrambled up and began to run towards the wrecked Battle. Others reached the aircraft first, and Yeoman suddenly felt his stomach turn over as he saw an airman reel away and sit down heavily, his shoulders heaving with nausea. As he drew closer, he saw the reason for the man's distress.

The Messerschmitt had placed a burst of cannon fire squarely inside the Battle's cockpit, blowing away the canopy. The pilot hung head down, half out of the cockpit, his back gaping open like a red-and-white flower. Behind him, the observer lay back in his seat, riddled with splinters, an astonished expression on his face. The gunner, in the rear of the cockpit, had no expression at all, because he had no head. His blood was already beginning to congeal over the rear fuselage.

Yeoman stood in silence and surveyed the carnage. He was horrified at his own lack of emotion. He felt no urge to be sick, nor did he feel compassion for the three shapeless lumps of meat which, just a few minutes earlier, had been vital young men like himself.

He just felt very old, and very tired. He had been at war for less than twelve hours, and already he was becoming a veteran.

# CHAPTER FOUR

A Messerschmitt was racing at him head-on. Tracers floated towards him. They were the colour of blood and they were converging on a point between his eyes. He could see the enemy pilot in the cockpit, and it was strange because he had no head. He wanted to bail out, to get away before the deadly tracers struck, but the cockpit canopy was jammed. He tore at it with hands that were bony claws. He threw himself against the side of the cockpit, screaming.

He was shaking and crying and there was a light in his eyes. He wanted it to go away, but it persisted. He put a hand out to push it away, and in that instant he came fully awake.

Callender was standing by his bed, holding a torch. Yeoman sat up groggily and rubbed his eyes. He felt awful. His mouth seemed to be filled with cotton wool and his head swam. The hangover from his nightmare had left him drained and weak. He was soaked in sweat. He looked at his watch in the light of Callender's torch; it was three o'clock.

'You were having a nasty one,' Callender said. 'What were you doing, making love to an alligator?' He thrust a mug of tea at the man in the bed, and Yeoman sipped it gratefully.

'Come on, abandon your pit. We've got orders to move.'

'Oh, God,' Yeoman said wearily. 'Where to?'

'Charleroi,' the other replied. 'The Jerries are crossing into Holland and the bomber boys are going to take a crack at them. Air HQ's raking together every available fighter for escort. The Battles took one hell of a hammering yesterday, and we don't want it to happen again.'

The fighter pilots did not know it yet, but the Battle squadrons had already been decimated. At noon on 10 May, thirty-two of them had set out to attack the enemy columns advancing through Luxembourg; thirteen had been shot down by the mobile 30-mm cannon that were accompanying the enemy advance, and most of the others had been damaged. It was this raid that Yeoman, Callender and Wynne-Williams had been supposed to escort on the way back. In the event, eight

Hurricanes from Nos 1 and 73 Squadrons had provided top cover for the bombers, but they had not met any enemy fighters.

The Battles had tried again in the middle of the afternoon, with thirty-two aircraft again attacking the columns of the German 16th Army in Luxembourg. This time there had been no fighter escort at all, and the Messerschmitts had pounced. Ten Battles had failed to return. With twenty-three aircraft destroyed out of sixty-four, and many of the others damaged, the Air Striking Force had flown no more sorties that day.

Yeoman roused himself, feeling better as the hot tea took effect, and swung his legs out of bed. 'It looks like being quite a do,' he commented.

Callender nodded. 'We'll be busy, all right,' he said. 'Oh, by the way — that's the good news. The bad news is that you, me and a couple of other guys are going to Charleroi by road. There aren't enough aircraft to go round. We'll be able to pick up some more up there, or so we're told.'

Yeoman grinned. 'Hey, that doesn't sound so bad. I haven't had a chance to take a look at France yet. A conducted tour sounds just the ticket.'

'You needn't sound so happy,' the other retorted. 'I'm driving, so you're in for a bit of education. These bloody Frogs won't keep to the left, you know, no matter how hard you blow your horn at 'em. Come on, out of it. You've just got time for a shave and a bite to eat before we get cracking.'

The Sergeants' Mess was on the top floor of an inn overlooking the cobbled main street of Ecury village, a mile up the road from the airfield. Yeoman, who had been warned that he would probably have to live in a tent, had been pleasantly surprised by the degree of comfort. The men slept two to a room, but the other bed in Yeoman's was empty; he didn't like to ask about the previous occupant, and no one seemed prepared to volunteer any information. A pin-up on a wardrobe door was the only evidence that anyone had slept there at all.

Hillier had stood down the squadron at dusk the day before, and there had been time for the luxury of a bath and a meal before Yeoman had fallen into bed. He smiled as he remembered his first meeting with the plump, motherly Frenchwoman who kept the inn. French troops who passed through Ecury knew her affectionately as 'Mémère', the English simply as 'Mum'. Rumour had it that she and Bert Duggan had more than a passing interest in one another, but if it were true they were very discreet about it.

She didn't seem to mind that 505 Squadron had virtually taken the inn over and furnished the bar as close to the lines of an English country pub as they could manage. She had taken the boys of the 'Cinq-Cents-Cinq' to her heart, treating the older ones like favourite brothers and the younger ones like sons. She had wept when they had broken the news to her that Simon Wynne-Williams was missing; but that night she had pressed his shirts and laid them neatly on his bed, as usual. 'Il reviendra,' she had told the others, as she dried her tears. 'Je le sais, au fond de mon cœur. Il reviendra, sain et sauf.'

The choice of the inn to billet the sergeants had been inspired, and they would not have changed it for any of the estaminets that littered Ecury — or the stately home further up the road that served as the Officers' Mess. The word 'Pelican' stood out in bold red letters on a large sign above the door, and although this referred to a brand of French beer and not the pub itself, it was the nearest thing the RAF men had seen to their own 'locals' back home. The Deer was above average, too, which counted for a great deal.

Yeoman got out of bed and lit the gas lamp over the wash basin; electricity was a luxury that had not yet reached Mémère's establishment. Callender went off to order breakfast.

There was no hot water, but he didn't mind; he was grateful for the cold splash on his face, and his razor blade was sharp enough to remove his stubble without too much discomfort. He dressed quickly, then picked up an empty gas-mask container that was lying in a corner and stuffed his shaving kit, toothbrush and some clean socks and underclothing into it.

He glanced out of the landing window as he made his way downstairs. Dawn was breaking, and it was going to be another glorious day. Outside, a blackbird sat on the branch of a cherry tree and sang its heart out.

Callender was already in the dining-room, tucking into a plateful of eggs and fried bread. Three other men were seated at the table; Yeoman recognized one of them, a flight sergeant pilot named Joe Shaw, but the other two were both flying officers and strangers. Callender introduced them as Jamieson and Wardell. The latter, a burly, fair-haired man who spoke with a pronounced Australian twang, grinned at Yeoman. 'We thought we'd gate-crash,' he said. 'You're a hell of a sight better organized down here than we are up at the château. No hope whatsoever of getting any grub before seven o'clock.'

'Ah,' said Callender, waving his fork in the air. 'That's because we occasionally deign to cook our own food. You have to descend among the hewers of wood and drawers of water to find out what hardship really is.' The Australian laughed. 'Some hardship!' He pulled a plate piled with thick slices of bread towards him, reaching for a jar of marmalade with his other hand.

Yeoman went over to the stove and helped himself to some food from the huge frying-pan that perched on top. The eggs had gone hard, but he suddenly found that he was famished and ate them ravenously, only half aware of the talk that went on around him. One thing did strike him; the informality that existed between the officers and NCOs. It was completely different from what he had been used to, and at first he felt slightly uncomfortable. Then he realized that differences of rank meant little to these men; they were operational fighter pilots, and that fact alone forged a bond between them that transcended everything else.

There was the sound of an engine and a squeal of brakes. A minute later, the corporal who had narrowly missed being vaporized by German shells during the airfield strafe the day before poked his head round the door, clutching his cap in his hand. He stared at the unaccustomed sight of officers in the sergeants' domain, seemed undecided about whether to replace his hat and salute, then decided against it and insinuated the rest of his body into the room.

'Transport's here,' he said mournfully. 'I've been detailed to drive.'

A roar of derision greeted this announcement. 'No fear!' Callender hooted, 'we're not going to submit our little pink bodies to your tender mercies!' He looked at Yeoman and winked. 'Henry here has suicidal tendencies, especially when he gets behind a steering-wheel. His progress is usually marked by a trail of broken fences, unsuspecting pedestrians and stray dogs. No thanks, Henry, you can sit in the back and darn our socks. The old master here —' tapping himself on the chest — 'is going to see us safely on our way!'

Henry looked unnaturally pleased. He picked up the pilots' kit and mooched out.

On the way, they passed a wizened old man who wished them a cheerful 'Bonjour!' His name was Philippe and he appeared, as far as Yeoman could work out, to have two functions in life. One was to stoke up Mémère's stoves; the other was to crank Ecury's ancient air-raid siren, a job that had kept him busy yesterday. He wore three or four First World War medals proudly on the lapel of his faded jacket. He was obviously doing his bit for France.

A battered Morris 15-hundredweight truck stood outside. Shaw, Henry and the two officers climbed into the back and promptly stretched out on some tarpaulins, intent on snatching some sleep — all except Henry, who sat near the tailboard, moodily staring into space and smoking. Callender got into the driver's seat and Yeoman sat beside him, studying an old road map which Henry had resurrected from somewhere.

Callender started the Morris and set off with a jerk, heading north-eastwards towards Châlons town. The morning was quiet, with no signs of war and few vehicles on the road, and as the sun rose higher Yeoman began to enjoy himself.

They passed through the outskirts of Châlons, taking the road that led to Suippes. Châlons had been bombed, but it seemed that the enemy had been concentrating strictly on military objectives such as roads and railways; there was little sign of damage in the town itself.

Callender kept his foot hard down. The road from Châlons to Suippes was reasonably good, as French roads went, and they passed only a few French dispatch riders and Renault staff cars.

It was not until they reached the crossroads just south of Suippes that they encountered their first real trouble. Callender careered round a bend, and the next instant there was a chorus of shouts and curses from the back as he stamped hard on the brake, throwing everyone brutally forward.

The Morris came to a halt inches away from what looked like a metal mountain. It was an enormous French 'B' tank, a 30-ton mobile fortress bristling with guns. Callender looked at his shaken companion, his breath exploding in a whistle of relief.

They climbed out of the cab into the middle of a crowd of gesticulating Frenchmen. An officer elbowed his way through; he wore a black beret and a captain's insignia, and his shoulder sported the flash of the 1st French Armoured Division. He looked coldly at Callender's stripes. 'Il y a un officier avec vous?' he enquired curtly. Callender jerked his thumb towards the rear of the truck.

The French officer's expression grew even frostier as Henry appeared, a cigarette dangling from the corner of his mouth and his tunic undone. He muttered 'Oh, Christ' and quickly disappeared. The Frenchman relaxed a little when Jamieson and Wardell emerged. He gave them a crisp salute, which they could not return as they were wearing no headgear. Wardell nodded instead.

The French officer spoke to Wardell in impeccable English. 'Please accept my apologies, but I must see your identification.' They all produced their ID cards and he nodded, relaxing visibly. 'I can see that you are in a hurry,' he went on, 'and I am sorry to hold you up. But as you can see, we have a problem here.' He waved his hand towards the tank. It was one of a dozen or so, jammed nose to tail. In front of them, French sappers were labouring to build a pontoon over a river. In fact, it was more in the nature of a stream, but its banks were almost sheer and it was plain that tanks would not be able to cross unaided. A highly accurate air attack had knocked out the existing bridge.

'How long do you think it'll be?' asked Wardell. The Frenchman shrugged. 'Who knows? An hour, perhaps two. We are heading east, but if you are travelling north I suggest that you take the left-hand fork here and follow the river for two or three miles. You will find a crossing point there. Unfortunately —' he smiled wryly — 'it is not suitable for our tanks, but you will have no trouble.'

He saluted again, then turned to his men as the RAF team climbed on board the Morris once more. Callender reversed for fifty yards, then took the road leading away to the left. As he did so, Yeoman caught sight of an aircraft, flying very slowly at treetop height about a mile away. It was a high-wing monoplane and looked like a Westland Lysander, the army co-operation aircraft used by the British Expeditionary Force, but he couldn't be sure. He drew Callender's attention to it.

His colleague studied the strange aircraft for a second, then swung the wheel hard and sent the Morris lurching off the road. He pulled up in the shelter of a clump of trees.

Jamieson's head appeared at the flap behind Yeoman. 'What's up?' he asked. 'Henschel 126,' Callender replied nonchalantly, fishing out a cigarette and lighting it. He looked at Yeoman. 'We might see some fun and games in a minute. That's a Hun observation kite, and if he's this far from the front I'd like to bet he's spotting targets. I don't want us to be one of 'em, so we'll sit. tight for a while. Stretch your legs, if you like.'

Yeoman got out and leaned against a tree, watching the Henschel. It turned and flew towards them, then banked hard and dropped down behind a line of poplars, the angry hum of its engine fading.

The minutes ticked by, and Yeoman began to wonder whether Callender had been mistaken. Wardell, who had joined him, read his thoughts. 'We'll give them a bit longer,' he said. 'It's my guess they'll be on their way, all right.'

Callender saw them first: a dozen black specks in the eastern sky. They were Junkers 87s, the famous Stukas, flying in 'vics' of three. The roar of their motors drowned conversation as they circled overhead. Yeoman craned his neck and watched in fascination as the leading flight seemed to check in mid-air, the dive-bombers peeling off one by one and plummeting down towards the broken bridge and the concentration of French tanks.

Yeoman would never forget the first time he heard a diving Stuka. Every aircraft was fitted with an underwing siren, a clever psychological move designed to strike terror into its victims. It rent the air with a hideous screech, a banshee wail that clutched at Yeoman's stomach with icy fingers. He watched the first Stuka pull out of its dive, and clearly saw a pair of bombs drop away. A moment later, the ground jerked violently, almost causing him to overbalance, and a terrific explosion battered his eardrums. A vast cloud of smoke and dirt rose from the direction of the bridge. With a sudden shock, Yeoman realized that it was just over a quarter of a mile away.

A hand struck him violently in the back, achieving what the concussion had failed to do. He sprawled at the base of the tree, with Wardell's shout ringing in his ears. 'Get down, you silly sod, and stay down! It's going to get hot around here!'

He was right. Stuka after Stuka plunged down on the luckless Frenchmen, pounding them unmercifully. A bomb, falling a couple of hundred yards off target, exploded just behind the trees where the RAF men were sheltering, showering them with dirt and broken branches. The rattle of machine-guns joined the already hellish din as the Stukas came in again, racing low above the road this time to strafe whatever was left at the foot of the mushrooming cloud of smoke near the bridge. Then they climbed away, forming up once more into their impeccable formation and flying back the way they had come.

Yeoman picked himself up, brushing away bits of grass and foliage. He looked at Wardell and indicated the pall of smoke. 'Do you think we ought to go back, sir?' he asked.

Wardell shook his head. 'What's the point? There's damn all we can do, anyway. If we meet any more Frogs we'll stop and tell 'em. Right now, we'd better get moving. That smoke cloud is a gold-plated invitation for any Hun who happens to be stooging around looking for trouble.'

More explosions cracked out as they returned to the truck. The shells were going off in the burning French tanks throwing debris high into the air.

Callender opened the driver's door, then stopped with one foot on the running board. 'Hang on a minute,' he said, 'where's Henry?'

They looked round. There was no sign of the morose corporal. No one had seen him since they climbed out of the truck. Wardell looked anxious. 'Let's search around,' he said. 'He can't be far away.'

He was right. A sudden crackling of undergrowth stopped them in their tracks, and they looked on in amazement as a white-faced Henry emerged from the bushes, holding up his trousers. He was covered in weeds and clods of earth.

'Caught with his pants down! Oh, lord!' Callender collapsed against the truck bonnet, helpless with laughter. Henry looked indignantly at the grinning faces around him, then climbed into the truck without a word, still holding his pants, his braces dangling behind him. Shaw sat down opposite him. 'Never mind, Henry,' he grinned, 'you've just proved something. Bombs are a good laxative.'

The corporal glared at him, his thoughts plainly obvious. Flight sergeants ought not to abuse admin corporals who handled personal documents — that was what he was thinking, with a fair degree of malice.

They drove on through Vouziers towards Mézières, encountering more congestion on the roads as they went. Their route took them through the reserve areas of the French Second Army, and the lanes were crammed with army units all heading eastwards towards the river Meuse.

A few soldiers waved and cheered as they drove slowly past — a process hindered by the fact that Callender insisted on driving on the left-hand side of the road wherever possible — but Yeoman noticed that most of the French troops seemed sullen and almost totally lacking in smartness. In fact, he had never seen anything so slovenly and poorly turned out, and said as much to Callender. Many of the poilus who trudged past seemed not to have shaved for days; uniforms were baggy and ill-fitting, with personal kit slung anyhow. Their transport was dirty, too, and antiquated. A lot of equipment was horse-drawn, and even the horses looked dejected.

Callender explained that the majority of the Second Army's troops were reservists, many of them in their forties, and from what he had seen of them during his six months in France their morale was appalling. He told his companion that not all the French Army was of the same low calibre; some units were very good indeed. Yeoman hoped he was right.

They had a heartening glimpse of the other side of the French military picture a few miles south of Mézières, when they were forced to pull sharply off the road to let two squadrons of Somua tanks race past. These were fast, 20-ton fighting vehicles mounting a high-velocity 47-mm gun. They were followed by half a dozen truck-loads of colonial troops, stem, dark-faced men from Madagascar who carried long knives in addition to their rifles and who would give little quarter to their enemies. Shaw summed up the RAF party's feelings:

'I'm glad that bunch are on our side.'

The congestion on the roads grew steadily worse as they moved north. It took them over an hour to get through Mézières; the narrow streets were jammed solid. A French convoy was passing through, and most of the population had turned out to cheer it on. On the other side of the town they picked up a dusty British dispatch rider whose motor-cycle had broken down. He was on his way to Nivelles, ten miles north of Charleroi; he had been through the rear areas of both the Second and Ninth French Armies, which adjoined one another, and his impression had been one of complete chaos.

'They've got no organization,' he told them, 'and their communications are hopeless. I was in Verdun for a couple of days before the balloon went up, and I'm not kidding — all the troops were working in the fields. Nobody seemed to be worried about anything.' He grinned. 'I'll bet they got a hell of a shaking up yesterday morning. Anyway, thanks for the ride. I'll be glad to get back to the BEF, I can tell you.'

By the time they reached the Belgian frontier it was already well into the afternoon, and they were all famished. The frontier posts were still fully manned, and the gendarmes broke into friendly smiles when they saw the RAF uniforms. They all went into the nearby guard hut, where the Belgians brought out bread, cheese and wine and insisted on sharing it with the RAF men. Henry, still maintaining a stony silence, made himself the hero of the moment by producing some tins of bully beef, which the Belgians ate with relish.

The Army dispatch rider spoke some French, and with his help the others managed to make sense out of what the Belgians were saying. They all thought one story in particular was incredibly funny. The day before, a detachment of gendarmes had arrested a couple of nuns who had been seen walking towards the frontier and behaving in what might be described as a furtive manner.

Following orders, two of the gendarmes had taken the nuns into the frontier post and ordered them to strip. The two elderly women had peeled off everything until they stood trembling and naked, their scrawny arms crossed over their wrinkled chests, eyes closed tightly as though to blot out the vision of their martyrdom. Nothing suspicious had been found on their persons, and the two gendarmes — both of whom were staunch Catholics — had been mortified with shame and confusion as they allowed them to dress again.

A good hour later, someone discovered that one of the nuns had left behind the bag she had been carrying. No one had thought to look inside it. It contained a Luger automatic, some fuses and detonators, and a pair of wire-cutters.

Not all the rumours, it seemed, were false.

They continued their journey, feeling a lot better with something in their stomachs. They kept a weather eye open for enemy aircraft as they drove northwards, but apart from a pair of high-flying machines which they could not identify they saw nothing. The Allied air forces were absent from the sky.

On this second day of the enemy offensive, 11 May, it had been the turn of the Air Striking Force's Blenheim medium-bomber squadrons to suffer. That morning, the Blenheims of 114 Squadron, based near Soissons on the banks of the Aisne, had been preparing to take off for an attack on the bridges at Maastricht when their airfield had been heavily bombed. The British aircraft had been caught on the ground, and the squadron practically wiped out.

Shortly afterwards, nine Fairey Battles of the tiny Belgian Air Force had also tried to get through to the bridges. Six of them were shot down by intense flak before they got anywhere near the target, and the puny 100-pound bombs of the other three failed to do any damage.

That afternoon, for the first time, the French bomber force was ordered into action. General d'Astier, still beside himself with frustration, finally received the desperately awaited call from GHQ, ordering him to 'put everything to work to slow up the German columns in the direction of Maastricht, Tongeren and Gembloux, and not to hesitate to bomb towns and villages in order to obtain the required result'.

The order came not a moment too soon, for d'Astier's colleague at Chauny, Air Marshal Barratt, had pitifully few resources left. It was, however, a forlorn hope. The most modem French bomber was the twin-engined Leo 451, and only ten were available to take part in the attack. They went in with a strong fighter escort and only one bomber was shot down, but the bridges were undamaged and all the other bombers were so badly hit that only one could be made airworthy within the next twenty-four hours.

Yeoman and his colleagues arrived at Charleroi-Gosselies airfield shortly before four in the afternoon to find the place stiff with aircraft, most of them British. There was a squadron of Gloster Gladiators and two squadrons of Hurricanes — No. 85 from the BEF's Air Component and No. 505. Hillier and his pilots had flown into Charleroi at noon and had already been in action twice, claiming a pair of Dornier 17 bombers and three Messerschmitt 110s for no loss to themselves.

The Hurricanes that awaited the newcomers were brand-new machines with three-blade Rotol propellers. They had originally been intended to replace the Gladiator Squadron's ageing biplanes, but had been allocated to 505 Squadron instead to make good its losses — much to the disgust of the Gladiator pilots.

Yeoman and Callender sought out their flight commander, Flight-Lieutenant Rogerson, who told them to get something to eat and then join the rest of the flight on 'readiness'. They lay beside their aircraft in their shirt sleeves, flying overalls and tunics having been discarded in deference to the heat, and tried to snatch some sleep.

Yeoman had just lapsed into a fitful doze when the drum-roll of bombing shook him awake. He scrambled up just as Rogerson dashed past, yelling '"B" Flight — after me!' There was no sign of any Huns, but there was a lot of noise coming from somewhere to the south of Charleroi.

Yeoman grabbed his flying helmet and climbed stiffly into the cockpit. An aircraftman helped him to strap in; another stood by with a trolley-acc, ready to start the engine. 'A' Flight was already thundering away, their task to patrol the airfield while 'B' Flight went after the enemy bombers.

The four Merlins started with a crackle. The sweating airmen dragged away the trolleys and chocks and the Hurricanes of 'B' Flight began to taxi, Yeoman keeping a careful eye on Shaw's aircraft immediately on his left. A minute later they were airborne and climbing hard towards Charleroi, over which the pilots could see ack-ack shells bursting.

They crossed Charleroi at ten thousand feet, still climbing. A lot of smoke was coming from the area around the railway station, in the south-east outskirts of the town.

They spotted the enemy suddenly, away to the left: nine Dornier 17s, heading east at about the same altitude as the Hurricanes. A careful look around; there was no sign of any fighter escort.

Rogerson's calm voice came over the radio. 'Line abreast — line abreast — go!' The four Hurricanes fanned out, their pilots opening the throttles. The Dorniers must have seen them, because thin black trails streamed back from their exhausts as they crammed on power.

'Number Two attack — Number Two attack — go!'

Yeoman selected a Dornier. Mesmerized, he watched tiny glowing pearls arc towards him from the bomber's rear gun position. The pearls dropped harmlessly beneath him, falling towards the Belgian countryside.

The distance between the two aircraft narrowed, and now the enemy gunner had his range. Tracers floated towards him, then zipped past his cockpit like angry hornets. Yeoman swore. His windscreen was icing up and he was looking at his target through an opaque film. He fired and missed. A slight correction, and his next burst shattered the Dornier's glasshouse cockpit. The return fire ceased abruptly.

He closed right in and systematically shot the Dornier to pieces, clinging grimly to the bomber as the enemy pilot tried desperately to escape. A sudden white trail from the bomber's starboard engine turned black, shot with vivid flames. An instant later the engine blew up.

Yeoman drew off and watched the Dornier's death agony. A black bundle fell away, tumbling over and over. Out of the corner of his eye, Yeoman saw the white puff of a parachute.

The Dornier's starboard wing folded up in a shower of sparks and debris, tearing off at the root and whirling away. The wreck of the bomber rolled over and went down vertically, trailing a sheet of blazing fuel. It hit the ground a few miles south of Namur and blew up.

Yeoman turned away, descending to five thousand feet in a bid to clear the ice that now threatened to obscure his vision completely. He pulled back the canopy with difficulty, for the runners were frozen, and revelled briefly in the blast of air that entered the cockpit.

The icing cleared gradually, and he headed back towards Charleroi. He felt no elation at shooting down the Dornier. It had been a completely impersonal act. He was almost too tired to care.

He was the first of 'B' Flight to land back at Charleroi. Rogerson and Shaw came in a few minutes later and congratulated him; they had both seen his Dornier go down. Callender had apparently been hit in the engine and had made a successful forced landing beside the Charleroi-Namur railway line. He turned up a couple of hours later, none the worse for wear, but swearing fluently and at great length because his bomber had got away. Rogerson had shot down two bombers and Shaw one. All in all, it had not been a bad afternoon's work.

Later, after stand-down, Rogerson borrowed an old Renault belonging to 85 Squadron and took Yeoman to look for 'his' Dornier, the bomber that had fallen closest to Charleroi. After a ten-mile drive they found the wreckage scattered around a huge crater in a meadow beside a stream. It was still smouldering. Some Belgian soldiers had already collected the charred and fragmented remains of the crew, for which Yeoman was heartily thankful. The sole survivor, he learned, had broken a leg on landing and was in hospital in Namur.

Rogerson picked up a souvenir: a fragment of tail-fin, two feet square and displaying part of a swastika. It was the biggest piece of wreckage they could find.

## CHAPTER FIVE

The Blenheims had never stood a chance. At seven o'clock that morning — 12 May, a beautiful Whit Sunday — they had taken off from their base at Plivot, a few miles away from 505 Squadron's usual airfield of Châlons, and had set course north-eastwards towards Belgium and the bridges at Maastricht. There were nine of them, and they all belonged to 139 Squadron. Since the disaster that had overtaken 114 Squadron the day before, they were the Air Striking Force's sole remaining medium bombers.

As they swept down to attack an enemy armoured column advancing towards Tongeren, fifty Messerschmitts had pounced and cut them to pieces. Only two out of the nine had returned to base, both of them badly shot up.

The morning had gone well for Joachim Richter. From dawn onwards, Fighter Wing 66 — together with three other Luftwaffe fighter wings — had been ordered to patrol the Aachen-Maastricht-Liège triangle, covering the bridges over the Meuse — the bridges across which General Hoeppner's 16th Panzer Corps was pouring into the Low Countries, the armoured columns spreading out over the drab Belgian plains.

Richter's first victory had been almost ridiculously easy. His flight bad been patrolling the line between Liège and Maastricht when suddenly three Belgian Air Force Hurricanes had appeared ahead of them, diving towards some unseen objective. He and two others had gone down after them. One burst was all that had been needed; the Hurricane had exploded in mid-air, its wreckage joined by that of its two fellows. It was doubtful if the Belgian pilots ever knew what had hit them.

Fifteen minutes later, north-west of Liège, they sighted the Blenheim formation. The British bombers were flying in tight vics, and held their course steadily as the Messerschmitts came curving down behind them. It was a massacre. Richter fastened himself on to the tail of a Blenheim and opened fire, seeing his 20-mm shells punch great holes in the bomber's green-and-brown camouflage. Within seconds the aircraft was ablaze from wingtip to wingtip. It reared up vertically, then fell sickeningly away into a spin. It slammed into a wooded hillside and blew up with a terrific explosion.

A terrific free-for-all developed as a squadron of Messerschmitt 110s arrived, queueing up in turn to harry the surviving Blenheims. The bombers were chopped out of the sky one after another. Richter marvelled at the tenacity with which the pilots held their course, right up to the end.

It was a jubilant crowd of fighter pilots who landed half an hour later at Norvenich, Fighter Wing 66's new base half-way between Cologne and Düren. Almost everyone had scored a victory, and they had suffered no loss during the morning's operations so far. Even Major Hartwig went so far as to slap Richter on the back in recognition of his two successes. Mölders had been right, the young pilot reflected. It was hard to believe that only two days earlier he had been almost ready to commit suicide.

Nevertheless, he knew that he didn't yet quite belong. He was conscious of the fact as he sat in a deckchair at dispersal, watching the other pilots of his flight playing skat. He had made the mistake of telling them that he had never played cards in his life; 'the devil's picture-book', his mother had always called them, and he had never had reason to doubt her. The others had just laughed, shrugged their shoulders and ignored him. It wasn't a very nice feeling. Maybe when he had a few more missions under his belt things would change.

A gangling, fair-haired youth wearing a first-lieutenant's badges wandered over and flopped down in a deckchair next to Richter. His name was Franz Peters, and he already had half a dozen enemy aircraft to his credit — including a pair of Wellington bombers, shot down over the Heligoland Bight in December 1939. He looked at Richter and grinned.

'Well, Jo, how's the war going?'

Richter smiled back. 'Pretty well, as far as I can see. We're making progress all over the place. How long do you think it'll be before we have the whole thing wrapped up?'

Peters shrugged. 'My own reckoning is that we'll be on the Channel coast in about a fortnight,' he said. 'I think that when that happens, the French will throw in the towel.'

'And we'll be in Tommyland inside a month!' Richter exclaimed.

Peters shook his head doubtfully. 'I wouldn't be too sure about that. A lot of people think the Tommies will sue for peace when we get the upper hand, but I don't know. They've still got a fair stretch of water between them and the rest of Europe — and don't forget they've got one hell of an empire behind them. No, you'll see — when Tommy's up against it, he'll get the gloves off, and then watch out! It'll be no picnic from then on.'

Peters swatted a fly that settled on his knee. 'Oh, don't get me wrong — we'll win in the end. All I'm saying is that this war's going to go on for longer than anyone imagines, and I'm not complaining; flying Emils is a lot better than working in a town clerk's office, which is what I was doing eighteen months ago!'

An orderly appeared with breakfast; sausages, rolls and butter, jam, and two flasks of coffee. They ate ravenously, with the appetites of healthy young men at the peak of physical fitness. Peters produced a silver flask from his hip pocket, winked, and offered it to Richter. The latter refused and Peters laughed, pouring a measure into his own coffee. 'It helps to keep the corpuscles going,' he said.

They were just finishing their last mouthful when the alert went up. Deckchairs went flying as the pilots ran for their aircraft. It was the same routine: patrol Maastricht at fifteen thousand feet. This time, the whole wing was airborne, and as they flew towards their patrol sector the pilots saw more formations of Messerschmitts, stepped up between ten thousand and twenty thousand feet, all heading in the same direction. It looked like being quite a show.

*

It was nine o'clock. Squadron Leader Hillier smoothed out the map that was spread on the wing of a Hurricane and looked at the pilots who were clustered around him. His face was grave.

'The situation,' he said, 'is bad. The facts are these: Jerry is pushing armour as fast as he can over two main bridges across the Maas, here —' his finger tapped the map at the spot where the borders of Holland and Belgium met — 'at Vroenhoven and Veldwezelt. It is imperative that those bridges be destroyed, but all attempts to knock them out so far have failed.

'The French Air Force and our own bomber boys are going to have another try this morning. Fighter cover over the target area is to be provided by 1 and 73 Squadrons and ourselves. The other two squadrons will try and prevent the Huns from getting through to the bombers, and our job is to deal with any that do.

'One word of advice — if you are hit in the target area, try and get clear before baling out. The whole area around the bridges is stiff with flak, and dangling on a parachute in the middle of that lot will be pretty unhealthy. Any questions? Good. That's all. Good luck.'

Yeoman was beginning to feel as though he had been born in a Hurricane's cockpit. There was an embryonic feeling about his presence there, surrounded by the familiar dials and levers, the rubber tube of the oxygen equipment and the tight grasp of the seat harness. It gave him a deep sense of security; he made his mind up that if he were hit, he would do all he could to stay with the aircraft and get her down in one piece, rather than bale out.

He had slept soundly the night before, despite sporadic bombing in the vicinity, and felt a lot better as a result. All his uncertainties and fears had vanished; he felt part of the team at last.

The twelve Hurricanes climbed steadily over Namur, flying in echelon formation, the fighters making a fine sight as they rose and fell gently on the warm currents of air,. The aircraft on Yeoman's left was flown by Shaw, who gave the young pilot a mock salute as he glanced across.

They followed the Meuse, curving gently over Liege where the river swung away towards Holland. There was a moment of alarm as six fighters arc'd down from the south, but they were French Morane 406s. The Moranes waggled their wings, then turned away and vanished in the haze.

A minute later a shoal of aircraft passed beneath them, flying north at about five thousand feet. They were hump-backed, twin-engined machines with twin fins and rudders and slender, tadpole-like fuselages. Yeoman was puzzled for a moment, then Hillier's voice came over the R/T: 'Relax, everybody, they're Breguets. All right, split up now. "A" and "B" Flights upstairs to seventeen thousand. "C" Flight, hold your present altitude. Orbit Tongeren.'

From a height of over three miles, the whole panorama of the battlefield was spread out beneath them. There was a lot of smoke coming from Maastricht and the area around the junction of the Meuse and the Albert canal. Hillier's comment about the flak had been no exaggeration; clouds of it hung across the sky, and as shells burst close to the circling Hurricanes Yeoman realized with a sudden shock that the enemy advance had already progressed further than anyone had thought possible.

A terrific air battle seemed to be raging over Maastricht. Yeoman could see tiny black specks dancing like midges over the town, and two or three black smoke-trails slashed across the sky like ink marks. Hillier, unmoved, ordered them to continue circling. The squadron of Fairey Battles earmarked for the attack on the bridges would be going in soon, and he was conserving his strength to protect them.

The flak Yeoman could see was directed at the luckless French Breguets, which were attacking enemy columns and being shot to ribbons. Up above, Morane fighters and a handful of RAF Hurricanes were fighting desperately against a swarm of Messerschmitts.

The voice of 'C' Flight commander, Flight-Lieutenant Rose, crackled over the radio. 'OK, we've got contact with the Battles. Turning in with them now.'

'All right, stick with them. "A" and "B" Flights, climb like hell. Let's get stuck in!'

The eight Hurricanes turned and raced towards the tormented stretch of sky over Maastricht, their throttles wide open. Yeoman felt a wild sense of exultation; everything was crystal clear, just as it had been on his very first air combat. He was flying number two to Flight-Lieutenant Rogerson.

It was the latter's call that warned them of danger. 'Look out, there's a bunch of the bastards high to starboard, turning in.'

'OK, got 'em. "A" Flight, turn to meet them. "B" Flight, continue climbing. Watch the sun.'

For long moments the radio was silent Then a barrage of voices broke in:

'Red Two, close up, for Christ's sake.'

'Watch out, there's more of 'em up top.'

'Red Two, break — a 110 behind!'

'Got the bugger!'

'"B" Flight, for God's sake get a move on!' Rogerson's flight was a couple of thousand feet above the mêlée now, and he brought his four Hurricanes curving down out of the sun. A Messerschmitt 110 fell past Yeoman, minus its tail. An instant later he flinched as an aircraft came at him head on, but it was a Hurricane. It flashed beneath him and vanished. A 109 streaked across his nose and he loosed off a short burst, but it was hopelessly wide of the mark.

An avalanche of 109s came tumbling down on their tails and they scattered wildly, hauling their fighters round to meet the new menace. Out of the corner of his eye, Yeoman saw Shaw's Hurricane suddenly disintegrate in a cloud of blazing debris, its wings peeling back like the skin of a banana. The shattered fuselage continued its flight for a second, rolling over and over, then dropped away below.

A 109 came at Rogerson from the port quarter. Yeoman stood his Hurricane on its wingtip and turned to meet it, firing as he came. He saw his bullets strike home on die enemy fighter's fuselage, then it was gone in a flash. He hauled the Hurricane round, the 'g' pushing him deep into his seat, and went after it. He caught sight of it a thousand feet below, in a shallow dive. As he plummeted in pursuit he saw the 109 turn eastwards, heading for enemy territory. With any luck, he would be able to cut it off.

Joachim Richter had felt the hammer-blow of Yeoman's bullets somewhere behind him, and had felt his guts momentarily twist with fear. Now, as he turned towards the sanctuary of the Meuse, he saw the Hurricane arrowing down towards him and knew that he wasn't going to make it. There was only one thing to do, and that was turn and fight.

He turned steeply towards the Hurricane just as Yeoman opened fire, sending the Englishman's shots wide. The Emil juddered appallingly as he continued the turn in a desperate effort to get on his adversary's tail. The controls felt sloppy, and with sudden brilliant clarity Richter knew that he didn't stand a chance.

A wisp of smoke rose between his legs, and paralysing fear seized him. He was sitting on top of the fuel tank. He was going to burn. The smoke grew thicker, blinding him. His frantic, groping fingers found the cockpit canopy release and the smoke poured out, streaming away behind. He had no idea where the Hurricane was. To hell with it. He had to get out, before the fuel tank went up and vaporized him.

He unfastened his seat harness and tried to lever himself out of the narrow cockpit. Something tugged at him, pulling him back. It was as though the Emil wanted him to die with her.

The Hurricane had pulled alongside. Through the smoke, he saw the pilot looking at him. The Englishman raised his hand, as though in salute.

He placed both hands on the canopy rail and pushed hard. The smoke was growing thicker all the time and he could feel heat against his legs. He put one foot on the instrument panel and gave a last, despairing heave.

The tearing hand of the slipstream caught him, hurling him along the side of the fuselage. The dark shadow of the tailplane passed over him. He was spread-eagled in space, clawing for the ripcord of his parachute. He couldn't find it. Panic choked him for an instant, then he forced himself to look down and search for the metal ring.

It was exactly where it ought to be. He caught hold of it and pulled. A huge fist knocked the breath out of him and his parachute deployed with an enormous crack. He looked up in alarm, thinking for a moment that something had torn, but the silken umbrella was in one piece.

He was swinging like a pendulum. He reached up and grasped the shroud lines firmly, then made sure that his feet were together. The swinging gradually stopped. He wrinkled his nose; he reeked of oily smoke. Apart from that, he found to his surprise that he quite enjoyed the sensation.

The roar of an engine disturbed his new-found peace. He looked up to see the Hurricane circling him, and his heart came into his mouth. He wondered if the Tommy pilot would machine-gun him. One had heard stories ...

He tensed himself as the British fighter suddenly turned towards him, closing his eyes. The roar of its engine reached a crescendo. Then, in a blast of sound, the Hurricane was gone, and Richter felt as though he had just been born all over again.

The faint rattle of machine-guns came to him from time to time as he floated down, but he could see nothing of the air battle that must still be raging somewhere above his head. For the first time, he looked down. There was a wood below him, but the westerly wind was taking him clear of it.

He hit the ground heavily, and his billowing parachute dragged him for several yards before he managed to release himself. He lay prone for a couple of minutes, painfully getting his breath, then sat up and looked about him.

He was in a pasture. A few cows wandered about, unconcernedly. A few hundred yards away he could see a low farmhouse.

A road ran along the edge of the meadow. A German convoy was passing along it. He waved, and a halftrack stopped. Soldiers descended and ran towards him.

A sudden shadow fell over him. He turned his head. A little Dutch girl, a pretty thing with long blonde plaits, stood watching him impassively. He smiled at her.

She spat in his face.

\*

Across the Meuse bridges, along the straight roads that led into the Belgian heartland, the Panzer divisions rumbled on, the sweating tank crews waving occasionally at the mobile anti-aircraft batteries that were springing up everywhere along the route. From time to time, smoke drifted across the fields from the wreckage of aircraft. Overhead, the flights of Messerschmitts roved incessantly, sweeping the sky.

Five Fairey Battles had attacked the bridges at Maastricht. All of them had been shot down. One, its pilot perhaps already wounded, had crashed into the western end of the bridge at Veldwezelt.

His sacrifice had delayed the German advance for exactly forty minutes.

\*

A young pilot officer sat on the grass beside his Hurricane, his face buried in his hands. His shoulders trembled. He was one of 'C' Flight's pilots. Yeoman looked at him.

'Anything I can do, sir?' he asked gently.

'Just go away and leave me alone. No. I'm sorry.' The other removed his hands and looked up, white-faced. 'Sorry. Don't take any notice of me.' He looked vacantly at the horizon. 'I never thought it would be like that,' he went on softly, almost to himself. 'It was terrible. There was just nothing we could do. It was the flak that got them — the Battles, I mean. They just went down one after the other.'

He stared at the ground. 'I saw one gunner trying to get out,' he said. 'There were flames everywhere. He was just like a torch. I could see him beating his hands against the side of the fuselage. God, I never want to see anything like that again.'

Yeoman walked away. How did one reassure someone who, only a few months before, had been a prefect at school, and playing cricket for the first eleven? How did one tell him that each time would be a little less horrifying than the time before?

Christ, he thought, you're getting callous, George. Three days in action, and you're as hard as nails already. He felt suddenly depressed, remembering the sight of Shaw's flaming Hurricane, and realized with a shock that he couldn't even recall the man's face. Was that how it was, he wondered? When you went down, did your friends forget even your face in a matter of hours?

Apart from Shaw, two other pilots had failed to return from the Maastricht show. Apart from one or two patrols over the airfield, there were no further operations that day. The rest of the squadron flew back to Châlons that evening.

Hillier was wise enough to see that the majority of his pilots needed some rest. Unless something big blew up, there would be no operational flying the next morning.

A truck picked up the NCO pilots and took them into Ecury just as it was getting dark. As the vehicle rumbled into the main street, Yeoman suddenly burst out laughing. Callender looked at him and raised an eyebrow. 'What's so funny?' he wanted to know.

'I was just thinking,' Yeoman said, 'that it's nice to be home. Up to now, I never thought of home as anywhere else but Yorkshire!'

As they climbed down from the truck, a plump bombshell burst from the front door of the Pelican, hugging and kissing each of them in turn. Mémère was in tears and pouring forth an hysterical torrent of French. They could make no sense of what she was saying.

They jostled their way into the bar and stopped dead, looking in astonishment at the remarkable figure that perched on a stool, surrounded by a group of laughing French soldiers. It wore a French infantryman's helmet, baggy pantaloons that appeared to have once been the property of a Spahi, and enormous boots. Most amazingly of all, it sported a filthy RAF tunic, on which a pilot's brevet showed up dimly. It grinned at the newcomers through a layer of grime and stubble, and the windows rattled with its welcoming yell: 'Ohé, les gars! Le vin est pauvre, mais il est frais! Venez boire un verre avec nous!'

Simon Wynne-Williams was back.

## CHAPTER SIX

The bar of the Pelican was crammed with uniforms, milling round in a sweaty press that forced the few unfortunate groups of French civilians into the shadows of the comers. Through the mêlée Mémère barged like a tank, trays of glasses and bottles balanced effortlessly on her upraised hand.

The party was in full swing, and so was Wynne-Williams. Washed, shaved and immaculate once more, he leaned with his back against the bar, recounting his adventures to a group of NCO pilots who were all in varying degrees of intoxication. Yeoman was no exception. He was half-way through his second bottle of wine and having some difficulty in focusing. He closed one eye and peered owlishly at Wynne-Williams through the haze of cigarette smoke.

'I still don't know how I got away with it,' Wynne-Williams was saying. 'In fact, I don't really know what happened. I think I collided with a Hun. Anyway, the last thing I remember seeing was some trees coming up at me.

'The kite must have broken up on impact, because when I came around I was lying quite a distance from the wreckage. No kidding, apart from this —' he touched a large bump on his forehead — 'I hadn't a scratch. They say only the good die young!

'I sorted myself out and started walking westwards. After a while I came out of the woods and spotted a farmer chap cutting a hedge. He told me the nearest village was full of Huns, so I thought I'd see for myself. When I got there, I found that the place was deserted. Everybody seemed to have packed up and gone.

'I wandered up the main street — come to think of it, the *only* street — feeling about as inconspicuous as a pork pie in a synagogue, when I practically fell over a bike propped against a wall. What's more, there was a long coat and a floppy felt hat draped over it. 1 took a quick look round; there was still nobody in sight, so I got all dressed up and pedalled off like fury down the road.

'I went on for a couple of miles and didn't see a soul. Then I turned a comer, and almost ran full tilt into the world's biggest tank. It had a great big black cross on its turret, so quick as a flash the amazing Wynne-Williams brain deduced that it just might not be friendly. There was only one thing to do. I put my head down, swerved round it and kept on pedalling. I went slap through the middle of a heap of tanks, trucks, halftracks, motor bikes, and God knows what. All the Jerries were sitting by the roadside, stuffing themselves full of sausage. They all cheered and waved as I shot past, and roared with laughter. I can't say I blame them. With my coat streaming out behind, and my big floppy hat down over my eyes, I must have given a passable imitation of a village idiot.'

His audience collapsed in helpless hysterics, the vision of Wynne-Williams in the role of village idiot proving too much for their alcoholic state. He lit a cigarette and surveyed them benignly.

'So you think that's funny?' he continued. 'Well, there's more. I went on for another few miles, with the road all to myself when I came to a crossroads. It was a very nice little crossroads, in the middle of a wood, but its beauty was marred somewhat by the presence of a German armoured column which was churning along right across my bows, so to speak.

'I couldn't run for it, because they'd seen me and a nasty big turret swivelled round and pointed its gun right between my eyes. So I stopped and did my village idiot bit again, drooling and crossing my eyes and hoping to God the Jerries wouldn't see my flying boots sticking out from under my coat. Fortunately I was covered in dust by this time, and that helped the disguise a bit.

'Anyway, there I was, drooling and simpering all over the place, with this bloody great gun pointing at me and me having bladder trouble, when the tank's skipper poked his head out and stared at me as though I'd come from Mars. And you know what the silly bugger did? He threw me a bar of chocolate and held up the whole bloody column while he waved me past!'

Wynne-Williams paused to allow his helpless listeners to regain some composure, and took a long swig of wine straight out of the bottle.

'Well,' he went on, wiping his mouth with the back of his hand, 'I pedalled off like old Nick was after me and didn't stop until dark. I kipped down under a hedge, and at first light I was off again. I'd jettisoned the hat and coat by this time, because it was getting pretty warm and I seemed to be out of Hun territory.

'I had no problems at all until I came to a village near the Luxembourg border. There were a few people about, but no one took the blindest bit of notice of me until this enormous gendarme shot out of a doorway and planted his flat feet in the middle of the road. I damn near ran him over. He started waving his arms and shouting, and I gathered that he was trying to place me under arrest. I didn't fancy the idea, so I smiled sweetly at him and laid him out. Then I took off up the road again with half Luxembourg in hot pursuit, all yelling and screaming fit to bust.

'A few minutes later I spotted a border post up ahead, so I ditched the bike and dived off through a wood. After about a mile I nearly fell into a river. I could see some Frogs moving about on the other side, so I waved and shouted. They didn't take any notice, so I stripped off and swam across. Trouble was, I nearly bashed myself senseless on a log half-way over, and lost everything except my tunic and underpants.

'As soon as die Frogs found out who I was, they bent over backwards to help me out. Their CO even provided a vehicle and an escort to see me home, as well as some togs. That's the escort, over there.' He indicated the soldiers who had been with him earlier. They were lying in a corner in various states of undress, sleeping it off.

The noise in the little bar was reaching shattering proportions. Clustered round a battered piano near the wall, a mixed group of RAF NCOs and French soldiers were on the eighth verse of 'Poor Little Angeline'. What the French lacked in words, they made up for by much shouting and foot-stamping.

Somebody pushed Bert Duggan forward. He was seized and hoisted on to a table. 'Come on, Bert,' Callender yelled above the din, 'give us your party piece!' Duggan raised his hands, looked blearily about him, and the assembly fell more or less silent. Then, in a rich and surprisingly tuneful baritone, he began to sing:

*It was in Anno Domini nineteen twenty-four*
*In the Kingdom of Basra there started a war.*
*HQ got excited and sent for Old Bert*
*To pull Operations right out of the dirt.*

His audience cheered wildly. There was a loud crash as someone dropped a tray of glasses. Duggan glared, took a gulp of beer, and launched into verse two.

*Now this bold bad rough pilot he sent out to bomb.*
*His bombs were OK but Ids tank was not full.*
*The AG behind the pilot did shout,*
*'You'll have no balls at all if your engine cuts out!'*

'No balls at all,' they roared in chorus, 'no balls at all, if your engine cuts out you'll have no balls at all!'

*They were just over Soom when the engine cut out,*
*And from the back seat came an agonized shout,*
*'If you land at the east of the Basrian Pass,*
*You might as well stick the Lewis gun right up your arse!'*

Duggan staggered and almost fell off his precarious perch. A couple of pilots grabbed him and pushed him upright again. He went on, undeterred.

*They looked o'er the side and was plain to see,*
*Sheikh Abdul Mohammed and his men were at tea,*
*Lounging around midst the sand and the rocks,*
*Discussing spring fashions and pruning their cocks.*

Yeoman, his face flushed, bawled out the choruses with the rest, doubling up with laughter as the verses got steadily worse. He felt strung up and light-headed; weary, but too tense to sleep. They were all like that. Drink was their opiate, and they would drink until they were past caring what the next day might bring.

Duggan finished his song and fell off the table at last. Someone cheerfully poured a glass of beer over him.

At the far end of the bar, a bearded French warrant officer was trying to get fresh with Mémère. When he refused to take no for an answer, she picked up a bottle and felled him with one expert blow. He subsided in a heap at the foot of the bar, and two RAF types threw him out.

A burly figure in an oil-stained overall shouldered its way through the door, blinking in the light and the smoke haze. Callender spotted the newcomer and called him over for a drink.

Flight Sergeant Len Thomas had been working non-stop for fourteen hours, buried deep in the bowels of his beloved Merlins. He crushed Yeoman's hand in a great hairy paw as Callender introduced them, downing a litre of beer in one go at the same time. He set down the mug and his vast belly rumbled.

'Needed that,' he said. He looked around, peering through the smoke. 'Hope you lot aren't getting too tight,' he said. 'I heard on the grapevine that we might be moving tomorrow. Don't ask me where to, but I've a feeling we're in for a rough passage.'

Callender groaned. 'I hope you're wrong, Len, but unfortunately you seldom are.' He waved a hand at the throng. 'This lot's going to take some breaking up. Come on, George, let's go and have a breath of fresh air. No point in trying to get our heads down with this racket going on, anyway.'

They collected Wynne-Williams on the way and wandered out into the night. It was warm, and the air was filled with a mingled aroma of dust and flowers. Yeoman filled his lungs, gratefully shaking off the smell of stale tobacco, and looked up at the velvet sky, picking out the shapes of the constellations. From the east came a dull, continuous roll of thunder, but they all knew it for gunfire.

They strolled on up the street, saying little. Yeoman noticed that there was no real attempt at enforcing a blackout; chinks of light showed from many windows. There was small wonder that the German bombers found little difficulty in locating their targets.

They stopped at the end of the street. Ahead of them, the road stretched away into the darkness, the poplars that bordered it standing out like black sentinels against the sky. Wynne-Williams lit a cigarette, shielding the flame in his cupped hand.

A loud crack sounded in Yeoman's left ear. He looked round, startled. Two more cracks came, in rapid succession. Callender grabbed Yeoman's arm and pulled at him. 'Get down,' he hissed. 'Somebody's taking a pot-shot at us!'

They dived full-length on the dusty cobbles. Cautiously, Yeoman raised his head and looked around. They had been standing in front of the whitewashed wall of a house, silhouetted perfectly for the benefit of the unseen gunman. He must have had a shaky hand, Yeoman thought, otherwise all three of them would have been dead.

Wynne-Williams tapped Callender on the shoulder. 'Make for that alley,' he whispered, indicating a dark opening on their left. They inched their way carefully towards it, then jumped up and sprinted over the last few yards. Another bullet hit the corner of a house, spraying them with plaster, and whined away into the darkness.

They flattened themselves against the wall, breathing hard. 'What now?' Yeoman asked.

Callender looked at him, his face pale in the gloom. 'I don't know, but I sure don't feel like sticking my neck out. I vote we push off, sharpish.'

They made their way through a garden at the end of the alley and returned to the Pelican by way of a series of back streets. Apart from alerting their own service police and the local gendarmerie, there was nothing else they could do. Yeoman lay awake for a long time that night, his mind seriously perturbed. Risking one's life in air combat was one thing; then, nine times out of ten, you could see the man who was trying to kill you. A bullet out of the dark, fired by an unknown, unseen killer, was a different matter altogether. Had the Germans parachuted snipers into Allied territory, he wondered, or were there Frenchmen who would actually welcome a German invasion and take an active part in helping to bring it about?

The next day, Yeoman learned that a military police detachment had picked up a suspect making his way northwards towards Suippes. The man's story was that he had been visiting relatives in Troyes when the Germans attacked, and he was now hurrying home to Lille to take care of his family.

They interrogated him for four hours, and he stuck doggedly to his story. He was only a poor labourer, hurrying back to protect his wife and children. His documents were all in order; why did the police not let him go?

They were almost fooled. Almost, but not quite. The interrogators had been studying the man's face; they ought to have paid more attention to his hands. They were soft and white and carefully manicured. No poor French labourer ever had hands like that.

They shot him that afternoon.

## CHAPTER SEVEN

Sedan, the old fortress town on the river Meuse, was the weak link in the French defensive line, and the Germans had known it all along. Here, at the vulnerable junction of the French Second and Ninth Armies between Sedan and Mézières, lay four of the French Army's weakest divisions, composed of fortress troops and reservists — poorly trained men, with little or no enthusiasm for their task.

Across the river, mercifully unseen, sheltering in the wooded valleys, no fewer than five Panzer divisions were poised to strike, to tear the thin defensive screen brutally apart. Behind the armour and shock troops, the roads leading towards the Meuse and Sedan presented an almost unbelievable sight to the German crews climbing away on their missions in the spreading dawn of 13 May. Packed nose to tail, churning slowly forward, was the mightiest concentration of armour in the history of warfare: fifteen hundred tanks moving in three great phalanxes. The whole column was a hundred miles long and behind it, still deep inside Germany, came the infantry divisions whose task it would be to consolidate the ground won by the Panzers.

The thirteenth, which dawned bright and sunny with a few shreds of mist clinging to the woods on either side of the Meuse, was the day of the Stuka. They came over in small numbers at first, attacking French forward positions on the Meuse and convoys bringing vital supplies up from the rear, operating in formations of six aircraft or less.

Then came the afternoon. On the west bank of the Meuse, the dazed French infantry cowered in their foxholes and stared in fear at the sky, the sky out of which the deadly gull-winged shapes came tumbling like an avalanche, rending the mind with the awful scream of their sirens. There was to be no respite for the battered troops. Even before the roar of the Stukas' engines had died away, more black shapes came crawling over the eastern sky; horizontal bombers this time, twin-engined Dornier 17s, droning across the river in serried ranks to unload their bombs with deadly precision into the pall of dust and smoke raised by the dive-bombers. So it went on for hour after nightmare hour, with successive waves of bombers pounding the area around Sedan before turning for home in an almost leisurely manner.

High above, silvery midges danced against the blue backdrop as French Moranes and Curtiss Hawks strove to harass the enemy bombers, only to be frustrated for the most part by the swarms of prowling Messerschmitts. From time to time, a black smudge in the sky or the wail of a helpless aircraft falling like a stone marked the end of an air combat.

For the pilots of 505 Squadron, 13 May was a day of utter frustration. While other AASF fighter squadrons were tangling with the enemy over the Maginot Line, they were ordered to fly a succession of patrols over the Air Headquarters at Reims. With the Luftwaffe committed to operations against the French defences, there was little activity further to the rear, and it was not until early evening that the squadron scored its first victories of the day when two pilots from 'C' Flight bagged a Heinkel apiece.

The pilots were roused at four o'clock the next morning, and Hillier briefed them on the day's operations. General Billotte, commander of the French Army Group One, had begged Air Marshal Barratt to send the remaining bombers of the AASF into action against the bridges in the Sedan sector, and all available fighters were required to cover the operation. French fighters would be operating at maximum effort in the area, too, and Hillier stressed the need for accurate recognition. Only the day before, two Hurricane pilots from the Air Component had cheerfully hacked down what they believed to be a Dornier; it had turned out to be a French Potez 63 reconnaissance aircraft.

Yeoman felt washed out. Although he had seen no action on the thirteenth, he had flown four sorties and had spent a restless night afterwards, his sleep disturbed by the continuous rumble of bombing. His eyes felt as though they were full of grit and his neck hurt abominably, making him wince with pain whenever he turned his head sharply.

Callender noticed him rubbing the back of his neck and gave him a word of advice. 'If you're having trouble, George, go and see the MO. You ought to know by now that you need to keep your head moving freely in a scrap, or you could end up in the soup.'

Yeoman knew that the advice was sound, but he had no time to act upon it. A minute later, the pilots were running for their aircraft as the order to take off came through.

Yeoman turned his oxygen full on as they climbed away, and the cool breath of the gas made him feel slightly better. He settled himself as comfortably as he could in the cockpit. Like the others, he had long ago discarded both flying overall and tunic, and now flew in shirt sleeves; his harness straps dug into his shoulders as a consequence, but that was a small discomfort he was prepared to tolerate in exchange for keeping his temperature down.

The Hurricanes climbed to ten thousand feet, heading eastwards to Verdun. As they approached the fortress town, a dozen blunt-nosed fighters joined them, holding a ragged formation a mile away to starboard. Yeoman identified them as Curtiss Hawks, nimble little radial-engined machines that had already given a good account of themselves in the air battles prior to the German offensive.

The whole formation turned gently over the fortress town, following the Meuse as it curved northwards. Ahead, in the distance, the river and the countryside to the west of it were obscured by drifting smoke, punctuated by the occasional twinkle of a shell-burst.

Suddenly, the French fighter leader broke away and dived across the front of the Hurricane formation, rocking his wings. A moment later, the rest of the Hawks went into a shallow dive. Looking down, Yeoman picked out six large, twin-engined aircraft flying a couple of thousand feet lower down. They were French Amiot 143 bombers, ungainly, outdated machines with fixed undercarriages. The situation must be bad, Yeoman thought, if the French were sending ancient crates like those into action.

The Amiots flew on in perfect formation, with the French fighters on either side. The Hurricanes stayed up above, the flights stepped up in echelon, weaving gently from side to side. There was no sign of any enemy fighters.

The Hawks broke away from the bombers and climbed steeply to port, curving round to protect the tails of their charges as they began their approach to the target area. The Amiots cruised on serenely, as though on parade. They were uncamouflaged, and the metal finish of their wings glittered in the sunlight.

Then, as Yeoman watched, the illusion of peace was brutally shattered. He blinked as a vivid orange flash enveloped the tiny metallic cross that was the leading Amiot. When he looked again the bomber had vanished, obliterated by the explosion of its own bombs. The remaining Amiots flew on through a storm of shell-bursts that erupted suddenly across the sky, holding their course. A second bomber faltered and dropped out of formation, turning over on its back. With sickening finality it fell into a ponderous spin. Two parachutes broke away, standing out like tiny white pinheads against the brown landscape.

There was a warning shout over the radio. An instant later, the Hurricanes scattered in all directions as twenty Messerschmitt 110s came hurtling down out of the sun. The enemy fighters continued their headlong dive, and the flak died away as they closed with the bombers. The Hawks had seen them coming, and the French fighter pilots turned to meet the threat.

'Maintain formation! Do not attack! I repeat, do not attack!'

Hilliers precise voice restrained the British pilots, who were itching to join the battle that now spread out beneath them. It was just as well. Fifteen more Messerschmitts came diving hard out of the east, and were on top of the Hurricanes almost before the latter had time to react. Yeoman, who was clinging grimly to Rogerson's tail, heard a sudden loud bang and saw a hole appear in his port wing. He turned steeply in the opposite direction, cringing in fear, and tried desperately to locate his attacker. He cried out as pain seized his neck in a vice, and felt sweat break out on his forehead. He kept on turning; it was the only thing to do. With a supreme effort, fighting the pain, he managed to swivel his head. The Messerschmitt slid into his field of vision, closing rapidly from the port quarter. The German was firing in short bursts, the battery of cannon and machine-guns in its nose twinkling.

Suddenly, a cloud of smoke enveloped the 110's starboard engine. The enemy fighter half-rolled and dropped away beneath. A Hurricane ripped past, and Yeoman recognized the code-letter on its fuselage; it was Callender, who had saved his skin just in time.

Another 110 appeared in front of Yeoman, weaving uncertainly from side to side, its crew clearly visible under their long glasshouse cockpit canopy. Yeoman kicked the rudder bar, his thumb hard down on the firing-button, and raked the Messerschmitt from wing-tip to wingtip as it skidded through his sight. Its twin-finned tail broke away and whirled past him; the remainder dropped like a stone. He caught a glimpse of the German gunner trying to struggle clear before the 110 vanished.

He got in another burst at a 110 that fleeted across his nose, and then his guns jammed. With a pair of Messerschmitts turning hard to cut him off, he realized that it was high time he made himself scarce. He pushed the Hurricane's nose down, opened the throttle, and dived hard across the river. Another painful look behind revealed the two 110s turning away in the direction of the Sedan bridges, where their colleagues were shooting the last of the hapless Amiots out of the sky.

The Luftwaffe had been active that morning. All along the route from Sedan to Châlons, columns of smoke rose from towns and villages which had been the targets of German bombers. Châlons itself had taken a battering; whole areas of the town were burning, and the sector around the railway station seemed to have suffered badly.

Yeoman's anxiety grew as he approached the airfield, over which hung a heavy pall of smoke. The Luftwaffe had paid a visit during 505 Squadron's absence, and the surface of the airfield was pitted with craters. He dropped his wheels and flaps and flew low overhead, surveying the ground. The only clear strip seemed to be on the northern edge of the field, between the canvas hangars — or what was left of them — and a deep ditch that ran along part of the boundary.

He made a steep approach, touching down with plenty of room to spare, and taxied back towards the hangars, weaving occasionally to avoid a crater. He shut down the engine, draining the fuel from the carburettors, and walked stiffly towards the operations hut, leaving his fighter in the care of a fitter and rigger.

The air reeked of high explosive. Henry, the bored corporal, told him that dive-bombers had attacked the airfield only a quarter of an hour earlier. Two airmen had been slightly injured, but apart from that there had been no casualties.

Yeoman suddenly felt ravenously hungry. Henry produced some bread and jam, and the pilot sat outside and wolfed it down, watching the other Hurricanes returning in ones and twos. He counted them as they came in to land, feeling their way cautiously among the craters. Two aircraft were missing, and most of the others were damaged.

Callender came over, humping his parachute. The seat pack was in shreds where a 20-mm shell had ripped through it. Fortunately, it had not exploded. 'Nearly lost the family jewels that time, George,' Callender grunted. 'Any idea who's missing?'

'I counted everybody in except two,' the other replied. 'By the way, thanks for getting me out of that spot of bother. Did you see the 110 go down?'

'Yeah, he made a hole in a wood. Did you have any luck?'

Yeoman nodded. 'Got a 110,' he said. 'I didn't see him hit the deck, but I don't think there was much doubt about him; he didn't have a tail anymore.'

Callender clapped him on the shoulder. 'Good show! That's something, at least. Christ, what a cock-up! Jamieson's had it; I saw him go down into the river. Those poor bloody Frogs really copped it; it was like watching a turkey shoot.' He kicked a tuft of grass savagely. 'Somebody ought to have his neck wrung when this show's over. We're running this damn war on a shoestring. The Huns hold all the cards. They're pushing their armour through like nobody's business. God knows what's going to happen when they really get moving; from what I've seen, the French have got precious little to stop them with.'

The other pilots drifted over, forming a sweaty cluster around Henry's tea-urn. Wynne-Williams had been nicked by a bullet on the forearm, and went off to have the wound dressed. Yeoman noticed that everyone kept a watchful eye on the eastern sky. Some of the pilots seemed to be in an advanced state of nerves; one man trembled so violently that he was unable to hold his mug without spilling the tea. He stretched out his own hands surreptitiously, glancing around covertly to see if anyone was watching. To his surprise, he was able to hold them rock steady. Somehow, the fact came as a comfort to him. He felt better than he had done all day.

There was little to do now but sit in whatever shade was available and await further orders. Fitters, riggers and armourers laboured under the sweltering sun, patching up and rearming the battle-scarred Hurricanes. Once a formation of aircraft cruised overhead, flying south-westwards; they were too high to identify, but there were a lot of them and everyone relaxed visibly as they flew on.

The hours went by, and still no call came for further action. Every half-hour Hillier telephoned Air HQ, requesting instructions, but the response was always the same; the squadron was to remain at readiness until further notice.

Over there, on the Meuse, General Heinz Guderian's Panzers continued to rumble across the pontoons into the bridgehead established the previous evening, while further north the 6th Panzer Division pushed through a second breach in the French defences at Monthermé, and in the Dinant sector the 7th Panzers under a young and talented general named Erwin Rommel poured into a third bridgehead. The French threw all their available bombers into an all-out effort to stem the tide, and they were slaughtered. They were shot to ribbons by the flak and the Messerschmitts, and by noon there were no reserves left.

At Reims, Air Marshal Playfair, the commander of the Advanced Air Striking Force, had been jealously guarding the pitiful remains of his light bomber squadrons. Now, with the French bombers out of action, he had no alternative but to commit his battered reserves to the fight. He did so with a heavy heart, for he knew that it would be a one-way trip for many of his young crews.

By one o'clock, 505 Squadron's labouring ground crews had managed to make eight Hurricanes airworthy. Half an hour later, the squadron was ordered to take off and rendezvous with a formation of Battles over Reims. Hillier split his available machines into two flights, leading one himself and assigning the other to Rogerson.

They picked up the Battles on schedule and set course for the target, the eleven light bombers flying at eight thousand feet and the Hurricanes four thousand feet higher up. The formation cruised steadily on, passing ten miles to the south of Mézières. Below the aircraft the ground was partly obscured by cotton-wool tufts of fair-weather cumulus, but the horizontal visibility was still perfect. The broad ribbon of the Meuse was clearly visible, with the dark patch of Sedan nestling among its wooded surroundings.

Apart from the occasional slender column of smoke, there was little sign of the battle that must still be raging on the ground. Yeoman, lulled by the drone of the engine and the whirling disc of the propeller in front of him, had to shake himself hard to get rid of a sense of euphoria. He had a strange feeling that nothing bad could possibly happen in such a setting, with some of Europe's loveliest landscape unfolding below. Surely, anyone looking down on it, whether British, French or German, could harbour nothing but friendly thoughts towards his fellow men?

'Red Three, close up!'

Who was Red Three? He couldn't remember. Funny how the rest of the formation was wandering about the sky. It must all be Red Three's fault.

'Red Three, close up for Christ's sake!'

His oxygen mask was dangling loosely by its strap, slapping against his chin. Slap, slap, slap. It was funny. He giggled.

The voice came again, insistently. 'Red Three, are you in trouble? Red Three, are you in trouble?'

He wished he could remember who Red Three was. The bloody idiot was messing everything up. Then another voice broke in: 'George, check your oxygen. Check your oxygen!'

George. Now there was a name he recognized. The voice that had spoken it sounded familiar, too. What was the other word it had mentioned? Oxygen, that was it. You needed oxygen if you were up high. But he wasn't up high, he was only at … funny, he couldn't read the altimeter. It was blurred, shrinking and expanding in front of his eyes.

He raised his hand to brush away the mist, and his fingers touched the dangling oxygen mask. Somehow, his dazed brain flashed a message to his fumbling fingers and he clamped the mask across his face. There was something else he had to do, but he needed another hand to do it, and both his hands were already occupied, one with the stick and the other with holding the mask. He tried to fasten the mask in place, and failed. He wrestled with the problem, sweating with the mental effort. Then he hit on the answer. Wedging the stick between his knees, he reached down and groped for the oxygen tap. He found it at last and hung on to it grimly, willing his fingers to turn it.

The instrument panel swam into focus once more as Yeoman gulped down the life-giving gas. He was trembling and felt sick. His voice sounded weak as he spoke over the R/T: 'Hello leader, Red Three calling. Sorry about that. I think I've got some fumes in the cockpit.'

A glance at the instrument panel showed that everything seemed to be functioning normally. There was no time to speculate on the nature of the fumes, for that instant a chain of flak bursts erupted across the sky ahead of the formation. The Hurricanes flew on through the tufts of yellowish smoke. More shells burst around them, the crunch of the explosions plainly audible over the noise of the engine. It was the closest Yeoman had been to flak, and he found it a frightening experience. He felt helpless in the face of these unseen shells.

The shell-bursts crept away as the German gunners turned their attention to the Battles, which had begun their bombing runs. Looking down, Yeoman thought that the bombers looked for all the world like flies, caught in a deadly spider's web of fire.

The leading Battle dropped its pair of bombs, which exploded alongside a pontoon in a twin fountain of spray, and jinked away to safety, pursued by rippling shell-bursts. The second aircraft was not so lucky. Caught in the meshes of the flak, it exploded in a cloud of blazing fragments that fell hissing into the river. Its crew had no chance to escape.

A third Battle completed its bombing run. Yeoman saw a pontoon burst into the air in a fountain of wreckage, and cheered inwardly as the bomber raced low over the surface of the water, away from the flak. Suddenly, it heeled over on a wingtip and ploughed into the wood that stretched along the river bank, exploding in a mushroom of smoke.

Hillier's voice burst over the radio. 'Squadron, follow me, line astern! Go for the flak!'

Yeoman saw the squadron commander's aircraft peel off and go into a steep dive, followed by the remainder of 'A' Flight. Five seconds later Rogerson led 'B' Flight in their wake, the Hurricanes hurtling down towards the glittering surface of the river.

The altimeter unwound with terrifying speed. Yeoman saw Callender's aircraft, two hundred yards ahead of him, pull up suddenly and speed above the river bank, smoke-trails streaming back from its wings as the pilot fired at some unseen target. Easing back the stick, he saw the long barrel of a 37-mm flak gun pointing skywards from the western end of one of the pontoons, and gave a touch of left rudder to bring it into his line of fire.

The surface of the river blurred underneath his wings as he streaked over the water at less than fifty feet. He had a fleeting impression of German soldiers throwing themselves from the pontoon as his Hurricane bore down on them, and of the gun crew desperately trying to traverse their weapon in his direction. Then his thumb jabbed down savagely on the firing-button, and the scene shivered as the fighter trembled under the recoil.

His bullets churned up the water short of the pontoon. A slight backward pressure on the stick, and he saw his fire blasting into the river bank, throwing clods of earth into the air. A gunner, his legs cut from under him, threw up his arms and fell into the water. Machine-guns opened up from the opposite bank, throwing up cauldrons of spray around the racing Hurricane. Yeoman sensed, rather than heard, the 'spang' of bullets striking home in his fuselage, an instant before he pulled back the stick and sent the Hurricane rocketing skywards.

He went up to four thousand feet and turned. The Hurricane responded poorly and the controls felt sloppy in his hands. He knew that he had sustained damage, but how severe it was he had no way of knowing.

He turned away from the river, glancing behind as he did so. The sky above the Meuse was a mass of flak bursts, with insect-like aircraft darting and weaving among them. Sedan was over on his right. Below him, a narrow road led south-westwards, out of the wooded hills and into open country. A strange vibration shook the Hurricane, a weird drumming that made his spine shiver. He throttled back to safe low cruising-speed, but the shuddering persisted.

He was finding it impossible to maintain height, and the Hurricane was becoming more insensitive all the time. He sensed that it was only a matter of minutes before he lost control altogether.

He toyed with the idea of baling out, but he was already down to three thousand feet and losing height rapidly. A forced landing seemed to be the only way out.

Ahead of him, the foothills gave way to a series of rolling fields, bordering the narrow road. There was a lot of activity on the latter; he spotted a few vehicles, but the traffic on the road seemed to be composed mainly of people on foot, so he thought it unlikely that it was a German column. In any case, he had no choice but to get down as quickly as possible.

He decided to go for a belly-landing. He picked the largest of the fields and began his approach, pulling on his harness to tighten it and opening the cockpit canopy. With the hood open, he would have at least a fighting chance of getting out if the Hurricane went over on its back.

He was already flying into wind, a fact for which he was thankful. To land downwind or across wind with only marginal control would have been to invite disaster, and he had not enough height left to make any wide turns.

At five hundred feet he switched everything off, trimming the fighter for the glide. Sounds impressed themselves indelibly on his mind; the sigh of the slipstream, the metallic pinking of the inert engine.

He crossed the dry stone wall that marked the field boundary in a flat glide, with plenty of height to spare. He resisted the temptation to push the nose down, to get out of the air fast. The field seemed to expand around him and he eased the stick back gently, raising the nose. The speed fell away rapidly as gravity took over and the Hurricane sank.

The jolt when the tail struck was surprisingly gentle. Then the fighter thudded down on her belly, careering across the field in a screech of rending metal and fabric. Yeoman hunched himself up into a ball, arms crossed to protect his face.

The Hurricane hit a ridge running across the field and bounced briefly into the air. It struck again and slewed round, shedding a wingtip. Yeoman was hurled forward brutally as the fighter reared up on its nose. For a long, agonizing moment it hung there, tail high in the air. Yeoman closed his eyes, convinced that the aircraft was going to topple over on its back. Then it settled, the right way up, with a spine-jarring crunch that knocked the wind out of him.

He groped for his harness release and unfastened it, shedding his parachute harness a moment later, and stood up painfully, bracing himself against the cockpit runner. The Hurricane was a mess, with only the cockpit and engine still intact. The tail had broken off and lay several yards away; the wings were crumpled and shattered. Yeoman shook his head, hardly able to comprehend that he was still in one piece, and levered himself out of the wreck, inhaling die fresh air gratefully. He still felt slightly dizzy from the fumes he had inhaled earlier; he would never know what had caused them now.

He took a few steps away from the shattered Hurricane and sat down, breathing heavily and feeling weak at the knees. A hundred yards away, people were milling around on the road. A small group broke away and ran towards him across the field, waving. He stood up shakily as they approached.

A burly, thick-set man wearing corduroy trousers and a vest was the first to arrive. Panting, he seized Yeoman by the hand and grinned at him. 'Aviateur anglais?' he asked. The pilot nodded, pointing to the roundels on the Hurricane's broken fuselage.

The man broke into a torrent of French, from which Yeoman managed to pick out a few words. The gist of it, he gathered, was that the Frenchman wanted to know if he was hurt. He shook his head. The other clapped him on the shoulder and spat on the ground. 'Ces salauds de Boches!' he growled.

They moved down the hillside towards the road, the Frenchman insisting on taking Yeoman's arm to help him along. His other arm was taken by a small, wizened man who sported a neatly clipped grey beard and a black beret. He tapped himself on the chest.

'I am Etienne,' he announced. 'I fight in the war of fourteen-eighteen. I speak English good. I am Sergent-Chef signaller. I liaise with 'Ampshire Regiment. 'Ampshire Regiment bloody good.' He winked. 'You trust Etienne. I help you.' He made a face. 'French Army now — merde! Not like fourteen-eighteen army. We know how to fight, then. But Tommy kick Boche up arse, you see!' Yeoman hoped he was right.

The road was crammed with refugees; men, women and children, moving in an endless column away from the thunder of gunfire in the east. It was the most appalling sight Yeoman had ever seen. It was the first time that the horror of war had been brought home to him; war that tore mothers and little children away from their homes and threw them, fear-driven, into flight.

He scrambled over a ditch and joined the human stream, wrinkling his nostrils as a smell assailed them: the smell of sweat and terror. He wondered, with a sudden sense of horror, whether this terrible scene could ever be re-enacted in England. It was hard to visualize, but not impossible. Suddenly, he knew with absolute clarity that he had a purpose in life. Hitherto, he had regarded the enemy as men much like himself, just ordinary chaps who followed orders; that was probably true, but behind those orders was a deep-rooted evil which had to be fought at all costs. It was an evil that turned these ordinary people into desperate fugitives because of one man's greed.

He looked at the faces around him, and read nothing but hopelessness. He stood by the roadside and watched them go by. An elderly couple passed him, the man bent almost double, dragging a small cart loaded with possessions. His wife walked beside him, her hand on his arm, the tracks of tears furrowing the dust on her face.

The dusty column walked on in a silence that was almost eerie, broken only by the rumble and squeak of cart-wheels, the tramp of feet and the occasional sob. Yeoman began walking too, flanked by Etienne and the burly Frenchman, whose name he never learned. He knew that the road he was on led to Vouziers, which he calculated was about fifteen miles away; there was an Allied command post in Vouziers, from which he ought to be able to contact Châlons. He hoped fervently that the defences on the Meuse would hold for a little longer; if they did not, it was very likely that the refugee column would be overtaken by German tanks.

A sudden cry jerked him out of his thoughts. He took another step forward, and collided with a young woman who had been walking in front of him, pushing an ancient pram piled high with belongings. Part of her load had fallen sideways into the road in a clatter of pots and pans. She knelt in the dust and scooped them up, bundling them into a blanket. Beside her, a little girl of four or five years old clutched at her skirt and began to wail. The tide of refugees split in half and flowed round them, never pausing in its weary trudge.

Yeoman stopped. Etienne tugged agitatedly at his arm, clearly anxious to be on his way. The pilot shrugged him off and bent down, helping the woman to collect her scattered things. He gathered up the bundle and placed it securely on top of the pram, smiling at her. She smiled faintly at him in return, nodding her thanks, the weariness and despair showing in her face. Yeoman appraised her closely and decided that she was a typical French peasant girl, pretty in a rustic sort of way, but with her cheeks and forehead already showing lines that denoted a daily round of toil in all weathers, and the anxiety of eking out a living from a meagre patch of soil. She wore a grey dress of rough wool, darned black stockings and unsightly clogs, but she held herself proudly, and the eyes that looked into Yeoman's were grey and steady. Her hair, what could be seen of it, was tawny. Most of it was hidden under a scarf.

The little girl was still crying. She was a miniature of her mother. Yeoman dug his hand into his trouser pocket, his fingers locating a piece of chocolate which he had put there earlier that morning. It was partly melted and sticky. He unwrapped it carefully and offered it to the child. She turned away shyly at first, but her mother whispered something in her ear and she reached out and took the sweet, putting it to her mouth and surveying the pilot with wide eyes. Yeoman laughed and took the child gently under the arms, swinging her high in the air and settling her on his shoulders. She squealed with delight, her mouth covered in chocolate.

They set off once more, the little girl perched on Yeoman's shoulders and the woman pushing the pram. Etienne trotted alongside, chattering away to her. After a while he turned to the pilot, wiping an imaginary tear from the corner of his eye.

'Her name is Chantal,' he said. 'She tell very sad story. 'Er 'usband is killed on Maginot Line in winter of thirty-nine. She work farm with father, but he die last month. She not have anywhere to go, now Boche come. Very sad.' He shook his head in sympathy.

Yeoman trudged on in silence, wondering how many thousands of times the girl's personal tragedy would be multiplied before this war was over. They walked for three hours without pause, Yeoman and Etienne taking turns at carrying the child. From his conversation with the Frenchman, Yeoman gathered that the Germans had been dropping leaflets over the border areas and putting out hourly radio transmissions for the past five days, all carefully designed to spread panic among the civilian population. It was not hard to spot the reasoning behind such a move. With the roads clogged with refugees, the Allies would find it virtually impossible to rush reinforcements to the front to contain an enemy breakthrough.

Yeoman's neck still pained him badly, and he quickly discovered that flying boots were not designed for long-distance walking. His toes felt like red-hot coals. He was glad of Etienne's company; the little Frenchman talked continually, apparently unaffected by the thirst and dust that caused Yeoman's tongue to stick to the roof of his mouth, and his cheerfulness helped to take the pilot's mind off his own physical discomfort.

They passed through a small village — or rather what had once been a village, for the bombers had been there before them. The place was a wilderness of shattered houses, the timbers of their roofs pointing starkly towards the sky. Stretching along the main street of the village, and for a hundred yards beyond it, was the remains of a French transport column. Some of the vehicles were still burning and smoke drifted up the street in an oily cloud. The refugees stumbled through it, picking their way round the wreckage, coughing in the acrid fumes. The human debris had been cleared away, but much of the transport had been horse-drawn, and here and there the poor creatures lay in twisted heaps, still entangled in their harness. It was a sickening sight, and Yeoman was glad when the village was behind them.

On the farther side, groups of French soldiers were sitting by the roadside, many of them displaying bloodstained bandages. Inert bodies, covered by army blankets, provided mute testimony of the effectiveness of the air attack. The troops seemed dazed and bewildered, staring blankly at the refugees as they shuffled slowly past One man stood in the road, spittle drooling from his open mouth, chin sunk on his chest, his hands making aimless fluttering movements; he was clearly deranged. 'Sauve qui peut' he kept muttering to himself. 'Sauve qui peut!'

His voice rose to a scream, following the refugees along the road. 'Sauve qui peut!'

Sauve qui peut. Every man for himself. That, reflected Yeoman as he tramped on, seemed to be a slogan that was sweeping through France like wildfire in this May of 1940.

It was late afternoon now, and scattered cumulus clouds helped to cut down the savage heat of the sun. Yeoman, in common with the refugees, was terribly thirsty, and it seemed like a godsend when the column reached a bridge that crossed a small stream. There was hardly more than a trickle of water, running between banks of dried mud, but the refugees flung themselves on it and drank greedily, filling whatever utensils they could find. Yeoman quenched his thirst and washed some of the caked dust from his face, feeling a lot better. Above all he wanted to bathe his swollen feet, but he knew that if he took off his boots he would probably not be able to get them on again.

The column moved off once more. Some distance farther on, they passed a signpost that told them Vouziers was still eight kilometres away.

They were all tired now and even Etienne had fallen silent. Yeoman kept looking back, hoping for a sign of military transport heading their way, but all the French army vehicles that passed them were going in the opposite direction. In any case, although the pilot might have flagged down a lift it was unlikely that he could have taken his two companions and the child along with him, and he felt obliged to see them at least as far as Vouziers in safety.

The little girl was fast asleep now, cradled in Yeoman's arms as he walked. Etienne came alongside and indicated that it was his turn to take her. Yeoman handed her over gently, sighing with relief and flexing his tired muscles.

He looked back yet again. The column was strung out along the road almost as far as he could see, the elderly and infirm having gradually been overtaken.

The fighters came out of the west, from a direction no one expected, diving out of the sun. There were six of them, Messerschmitt 109s, and they blasted over the heads of the refugees like a whirlwind. Everything happened in seconds, but to Yeoman time seemed to hang suspended. He screamed at those nearest to him to get off the road and lie flat. They looked at him un-comprehendingly. He pushed at Chantal and Etienne. The woman tried to drag her laden pram with her and the pilot pulled her harshly away from it. The next instant he was almost trampled underfoot by a horde of screaming, panic-stricken people as the fighters returned, streaking along the road from the opposite direction and firing as they came. The woman was swept away from him. He tried to reach out to her and fell headlong, striking his forehead painfully against a cart-wheel. A line of machine-gun fire exploded along the surface of the road, throwing up a whirlwind of dust and stones. People fell screaming, thrashing in agony as the bullets cut into them.

Horrified, Yeoman raised his head and saw Chantal's little girl, running up the road with short, uncertain steps. Somehow, she had struggled clear of Etienne's arms. She wailed in terror. Yeoman struggled to his feet and lunged towards her as another Messerschmitt came boring in, the bark of its cannon and machine-guns drowning the nightmare cries of pain and fear.

In front of the pilot, a small figure rose from a cluster of sprawled bodies. It was Etienne. Blood poured from a wound in his shoulder; his beret had gone and his white hair streamed out as he hurled himself on the child, bearing her to the ground and covering her with his body.

A burst of fire missed Yeoman's pounding feet by inches. He cried out in horror as the bullets tracked across Etienne. The little Frenchman jerked once and then was still.

The Messerschmitts flew away. Yeoman stumbled forward and knelt beside Etienne, trying to shut his ears to the gasps and moans of the wounded and dying. Tenderly, he turned the Frenchman over. Blood poured over his hands. Etienne opened his eyes. There was a kind of wonder in them. He smiled, tried to say something, and died.

The little girl was senseless, but otherwise unharmed. Yeoman picked her up from the dusty, bloodstained surface of the road. He walked back slowly to the spot where Chantal's pram lay overturned, its contents strewn around it. Tears poured down his face, and he was not ashamed of them.

He stopped and looked down with infinite sadness. Chantal lay face down, her face resting on the grass verge. Her head scarf had come loose, and the light breeze played with her hair. There were three crimson holes in her back, and she was dead.

You bastards, Yeoman cursed silently. You rotten, filthy bastards. He turned and walked away, stepping carefully round the tumbled bodies in the road, holding the still-unconscious child close to him. He wanted to put the scene of carnage behind him as quickly as possible. There would be others to bury the dead. He had a score to settle with the living.

He strode on, losing count of the time. The child came round and clung to him. She made no murmur, and seemed unaware of her surroundings. Yeoman was grateful. She was such a tiny thing. She would know grief, when the shock wore off, but it would soon pass. The girl who had borne her and cared for her would be wraith-like in her mind, almost, but never quite, forgotten.

He walked on for an hour, leaving the survivors of the refugee column far behind. His feet were hurting badly, and his spirits rose when he heard the sound of an engine, approaching from behind.

He planted himself in the middle of the road and faced the oncoming vehicle. It was a Renault staff car, and the driver blew his horn furiously as it drew nearer. Yeoman held up his hand and the car screeched to a stop with only a couple of feet to spare.

Yeoman moved round to the driver's window and peered in. The driver was a very young French soldier who appeared to be suffering from a bad attack of nerves. Next to him sat an elderly colonel with a florid complexion and a waxed moustache, who barked at Yeoman through the open window. It was clear that the French officer was highly displeased by this unexpected interruption of his journey.

Yeoman ignored him. He was looking at the occupant of the back seat. She was, he judged, in her mid-twenties, and she was one of the most elegant women he had ever seen. Her red hair fell in a cascade around her shoulders, framing a long, fine face from which a pair of translucent green eyes appraised Yeoman boldly. She wore a blue silk dress and sat back at her ease, slender legs crossed, smoking casually. A leather suitcase lay beside her on the seat.

Yeoman tore his gaze away from her and addressed the colonel, groping for the right words in his halting French.

'Je suis aviateur anglais,' he said. 'Je suis — je suis — shot down.' He made a descending motion with his free hand. 'Je vais à Châlons avec la petite fille. Sa mère est morte. Nous voulons aller avec vous.'

It was not the most polite of requests, but it was the best he could manage. It wasn't good enough for the colonel. He waved Yeoman away with an imperious gesture and ordered the driver to continue.

When he had taken off that morning, Yeoman had pushed his Smith and Weston .38 revolver into the top of his right flying boot. Often, during the march westwards, he had been going to throw it away because it chafed his leg, but he had resisted the temptation — not because he thought be might need it, but because he knew that he would have to account for it if he lost it. It certainly came in handy now. He dragged it out and pushed the muzzle into the colonel's ear.

'All right, you fat bastard,' he ground out, 'I don't know if you can understand me or not, but this whole bloody set-up looks fishy to me. You ought to be going towards the fighting, not away from it. I'm going with you as far as Châlons, and if I have any trouble from you I'll blow your bloody head off!'

The colonel turned white and his mouth dropped open. Yeoman gave him no time to argue. Setting down the child briefly, he opened the rear passenger door of the car, bundling the little girl inside and following her quickly. He prodded the driver in the back of the neck with the gun. Trembling, the man put the car into gear and moved off.

'That was well done, but not really necessary. The old slob thinks he's going to sleep with me tonight; I wouldn't have let him leave you behind.'

The voice was cultured, and American. Yeoman turned in astonishment and looked at the redhead. She smiled at him and held out her hand. 'Julia Connors,' she said. 'Correspondent, *New York Globe.*' The pilot gathered his wits. 'George Yeoman,' he told her. 'Sergeant Pilot, Royal Air Force.'

She laughed. 'Lost your aeroplane, I see.' She reached down and stroked the child's hair. 'How come you've got the kid in tow?'

Briefly, Yeoman told his story. When he had finished Julia sat in silence for a few moments, her face grim. She lit another cigarette, then stubbed it out savagely. 'Christ, what shits those people are!'

Yeoman nodded. 'It's funny, though,' he said, 'I can't bring myself to hate them. Most of them are just ordinary blokes like me, doing a pretty rotten job. If I have any hatred at all, it's for the politicians and that includes our lot — the ones who let all this happen.' 'What are you going to do now?' Julia wanted to know.

'I need to get to Châlons as quickly as possible,' he told her. 'I can leave the little girl with Mémère — that's the friendly soul who runs the inn where we are billeted. I just hope the squadron hasn't moved. They probably think I've had it.'

She offered him a cigarette, which he refused. 'What about you?' he asked. 'How do you come to be mixed up in all this?'

'Oh, I've been in France since last December. You might think it a bit strange to find a female as a war correspondent, but believe me it pays dividends. I've managed to get hold of stories a guy wouldn't have got near, just because old fools like that —' she waved a hand contemptuously towards the colonel — 'can't keep their mouths shut when they see a pair of legs. No wonder the Germans knew everything there was to know about their defences.'

Yeoman looked at her questioningly. 'So it was pretty bad up front?' he asked. She made a face.

'Worse. I toured the whole of the Maginot Line from end to end, and saw things you wouldn't believe. Bungling and incompetence and graft — officers and senior NCOs getting fat on the proceeds from government stores — soldiers planting cabbages instead of doing weapon training — my God, it was appalling. Morale was non-existent, and the few officers who did try to instil some pride into their men soon gave it up as a bad job and took to socializing with the local high society instead. If France could win the war on champagne and cognac, she'd have no problem.'

'The Germans certainly seemed to be making headway when last I saw them,' Yeoman observed.

'You're not kidding. They're breaking through all over the place. I got orders to move out fast when the attack started, but I hung on as long as I could. Old fatty here jumped at the chance to drive me back to the rear under his personal escort; he'd probably have crawled away from the front on his hands and knees if he'd had to.'

They passed straight through Vouziers and took the road to Suippes, finding progress slower as they encountered transport columns moving up towards the front Once they were stopped by French field security police. At Yeoman's request, Julia willingly told the French colonel not to make any trouble; the pressure of the pilot's gun muzzle through the back of his seat was all the persuasion he needed. The checkpoint was passed without incident.

It was well after dark when they arrived at Châlons. They drove straight through the town to Ecury. On the outskirts of the village, Yeoman ordered the driver to stop. He lifted the child, who was asleep once more, and climbed out of the car, still brandishing the revolver. Julia got out too, pulling her suitcase behind her. 'Hold on,' she said, 'this is where I say farewell to Marshal Foch here. The RAF has hereby got itself an unofficially accredited correspondent.' Yeoman looked at her in the gloom, knowing determination when he saw it. It was useless to protest. He waved his revolver and the staff car moved off up the street, gathering speed rapidly.

They watched it until it was out of sight. 'I hope he doesn't make trouble,' the pilot grunted.

Julia laughed. 'I shouldn't worry about him. He's too interested in saving his own skin. I'd like to bet he doesn't stop until he reaches Paris. No doubt he'll find another plausible story to account for his absence from the front.'

The village seemed deserted. They walked slowly towards the Pelican, picking their way carefully among piles of rubble. Even in the darkness, Yeoman could see that several houses had been demolished. It looked as though Ecury had received a stick of bombs.

The Pelican, thankfully, seemed intact. Yeoman hammered on the door. After what seemed an age, he heard sounds of movement inside. The door opened a few inches and Mémère stood on the threshold, shielding a candle. Her mouth fell open in astonishment.

Yeoman suddenly felt desperately weary. His head swam and he swayed, seeing Mémère's face blurring in front of him. He thrust the sleeping child into the startled woman's arms and pushed past her, leaning against the wall for support. His last impression, in the flickering light of the candle, was of the threadbare carpet on the hall floor coming up to meet him.

## CHAPTER EIGHT

He opened his eyes reluctantly. Julia was shaking him, looking concerned. He felt awful. 'What time is it?' he grunted, wriggling his toes. Someone had removed his boots.

'It's four o'clock,' she replied. 'In the morning, I mean. Come on, we've got to get moving. Here, drink this.' She thrust a mug of coffee into his hands. There was more than a dash of cognac in it. He felt the warmth creep down to his stomach.

He surveyed her groggily. She had discarded her silk dress in favour of slacks, blouse and a short jacket. Her hair was tied back. 'You've changed,' he said.

She laughed. 'Ten out of ten for observation. I've been trying to wake you for ages; you must have been really worn out. Listen, there's no time to lose. The Germans are in Rethel already. Some French troops passed through a while ago with the news. The enemy armour is pushing west and south, which probably means it'll be here sometime today. We've got to get out.'

'I have to report to the squadron,' Yeoman said. 'Should have done it last night.'

'Your squadron's not here anymore,' Julia told him. 'I've been talking to Mémère. They left a few guys at the airfield for demolition, though; with a bit of luck we can catch them and find out where the rest have gone. Come on, you've got five minutes to freshen up. I've organized some transport.'

Yeoman got up stiffly. 'You astonish me,' he said. 'Born to command, you are. It makes me feel quite inferior.'

She grinned at him. 'Don't let it worry you. Haven't you heard about the all-American woman? An incredible species. We started wearing trousers when it got chilly on the *Mayflower*, and we haven't taken 'em off since.'

Her cheerful humour had a tonic effect on the pilot. He went upstairs and washed quickly, then opened the door of his wardrobe and looked in. His kit had gone, presumably collected by one of his colleagues, but his roll-neck sweater was still there, bundled into a corner. He picked it up and tucked it under his arm. The nights could be pretty cold, and it would come in useful if he had to rough it.

He paused at the door and took a last look round, recalling with something of a shock that it was only five days since he had first entered the little room. Since then, the cockpit of his Hurricane had been more of a home to him. Nevertheless, he felt a sense of loss at leaving. He could not help wondering whether he would ever see the Pelican again.

Julia and Mémère were waiting for him at the foot of the stairs. Julia was holding a bulging shoulder bag and a napkin full of food, which Mémère had pressed upon her. The plump Frenchwoman burst into tears and hugged Yeoman tightly, trying hard to get words out between her sobs. 'She says you are not to worry about little Celine,' Julia told him. 'She'll look after her and treat her just like her own child.' It was the first time Yeoman had heard the little girl's name. Thankfully, he knew that he couldn't have wished to leave her with a better foster-mother.

Mémère kissed them both warmly. Yeoman realized suddenly that she must be going through a great deal of personal agony. She had lived through one German occupation; now the terror of another was about to descend upon her.

Julia tugged urgently at him. 'Let's get going,' she said urgently. 'The sun's up.'

He squeezed the Frenchwoman's arm and turned away, following Julia outside. She paused on the threshold. 'Well,' she said, pointing, 'there it is.'

A motor-cycle stood by the door. It was by no means new, but a quick inspection showed him that it was in reasonable order. 'Good God,' he exclaimed, 'where did you dig that up from?'

'Apparently it belonged to Mémère's cousin. He got called up a few months ago. I didn't want to take it, but she insisted. She says she'll make it all right with him when he gets back. Like it?'

'Do I like it? It's bloody fantastic! Tell Mémère I love her.' He swung a leg over the saddle and kicked the engine into life. He yelled at Julia above the noise, and she mounted the pillion. They waved at Mémère, who was standing in the doorway dabbing her eyes. Then they were away in a blare of sound that made the Pelican's tiles rattle.

Mémère leaned wearily against the doorpost and watched as they rounded the corner at the end of the street, the noise of their engine lingering for a long time after they had vanished from sight. She stood there for long minutes, feeling a sense of desolation. Then she roused herself and went inside. The little girl was whimpering in her sleep. Mémère went upstairs to where the child lay snugly in the landlady's bed. She reached down, tenderly stroking the little girl's hair. Life still had a purpose.

Yeoman opened the throttle and sent the bike leaping along the narrow road, revelling in the sensation of power and the cool rush of the morning air against his face. Julia's arms were tight around his waist and he heard her laugh out loud with sheer pleasure as they sped on, the hedgerows blurring on either side.

The breeze brought the smell of burning to them as they approached the airfield. Yeoman slowed down, turning off the road and up the narrow track that led to where the canvas hangars had been. They were no longer there. Everything had been taken apart, piled into a great bonfire and burned. Alongside, the skeletons of two Hurricanes still smouldered.

The field was not completely deserted. On the far side, in the shadow of a clump of trees, Yeoman picked out the outline of a camouflaged truck. He bumped towards it across the grass; it was an old Fordson tender, with what looked like a couple of radio aerials sticking out of the roof.

He swung across the grass towards it, skirting the profusion of bomb craters. He was fifty yards from the truck when he heard the report of a rifle and the simultaneous crack of a bullet, cleaving the air a few feet above his head. He swerved violently, almost throwing Julia from her seat, and stopped. He switched off the engine and slowly raised his hand. He knew that whoever was in the tender could have killed him easily, had he wanted to.

A man emerged from behind the tender. To his relief, Yeoman saw that he wore RAF uniform. He also carried a Lee-Enfield rifle, which was pointing unwaveringly in the pilot's direction.

'All right,' he shouted, 'that's far enough. Get off that thing and come over here. The woman as well.'

Yeoman and Julia did as they were told. As they got closer, they saw that the man was a corporal, the flash on his sleeve denoting that he was also a signaller. He looked tired and drawn, and in no mood for any funny business.

'The name's Yeoman,' the pilot told him. 'Sergeant, 505 Squadron. Got shot down over the Meuse yesterday and I'm looking for my unit. No identification, I'm afraid, apart from my disc. This is Miss Connors, American war correspondent. She's been giving me a bit of a hand.'

The corporal looked unimpressed, but he lowered the rifle muzzle slightly, as though uncertain what to do. 'It all sounds funny to me,' he muttered.

The trio stood in an uneasy silence, with Yeoman racking his brains for some way of convincing the NCO that he and his companion were genuine. The man was clearly in a state of nerves. Any false move might result in tragedy.

'Hang on, he's all right. I know him.'

Startled, Yeoman looked round. Wandering towards them, hands in pockets, as scruffy and morose as ever, was Henry. He raised an eyebrow. 'Thought you were dead,' he said.

Yeoman almost laughed aloud in sheer relief. 'Am I glad to see you! I thought this bloke was going to give us ten yards start and then start shooting.' The corporal had lowered his rifle now and was grinning, obviously every bit as relieved as Yeoman.

Yeoman wanted to know what was happening. Henry shrugged. 'I'm dog's-body as usual,' he complained. 'They left me behind to give this bloke here a hand, packing up his radio gear. We're supposed to catch up with the squadron. They've pulled back to Creil.'

'Where the hell's that?' Yeoman asked.

'About twenty miles north of Paris. Hold on, I'll show you.' Henry went inside the tender and produced a map. Yeoman studied it, memorizing the route. It seemed straightforward enough.

'Listen, Henry,' he said, 'if I were you I'd get going as soon as you can. The Huns are on their way here. We'll stick with the motor-bike, because it's faster. I want to drop Miss Connors off in Paris and get back to the unit as soon as I can. One pilot might not make that much difference, but every little helps, as the old woman said who peed in the sea. Look after yourselves, and don't get caught. Come on, Julia.'

They ran back to the motor-cycle. As they moved away, Yeoman glanced back. The two men were climbing into their truck. With any luck, they would be well on their way before the Germans arrived. He grinned to himself. If anyone was going to come out of this business with a whole skin, he thought, it would be Henry. The little corporal was made for survival, despite his offhand appearance.

A few hours later, a lone Henschel 126 observation aircraft appeared over Châlons. It circled the airfield several times. The pilot and his observer, seeing no sign of life, touched down on the grass and got out to make a closer inspection. Satisfied, they took off once more and flew away eastwards.

Early that evening, the little village of Ecury trembled to the roar of engines. The inhabitants, those who remained, came to their doors and peered apprehensively into the sky. Low overhead thundered a formation of Stuka dive-bombers, their silhouettes black and menacing against the clouds. A few minutes behind them came four lumbering Junkers 52 transports, carrying support personnel.

The Stukas went into line astern and curved down to land at Châlons, taxiing past the burnt-out Hurricanes and dispersing around the airfield perimeter. The Junkers also touched down, disgorging ground crews and stores, before taking off again. The dive-bomber crews stayed beside their aircraft, awaiting the arrival of the Luftwaffe column which, with armoured support, had been breaking all records to keep up with them.

The first Panzers rumbled on to the airfield ninety minutes later.

## CHAPTER NINE

Paris was just as Yeoman had always imagined it, with its broad, tree-lined avenues and landmarks which, although new to him at first hand, somehow seemed familiar.

Thanks to Julia, the journey from Châlons had been uneventful. Whenever they had been challenged, her fluent French and her credentials had seen them through. If he had been on his own, Yeoman reflected, it would probably have been a very different story.

Because of the hold-ups and the congested roads, it took them over three hours to cover the seventy miles to the French capital. They arrived with petrol to spare, stopping at a cafe in the suburbs to telephone their respective embassies. After some consultation, an official at the British Embassy promised to contact Yeoman's squadron with the news that the pilot was safe. Transport to Creil, he said, might be arranged if the pilot reported to the embassy in two hours' time.

They ordered a cool beer apiece and fell gratefully into wicker chairs at one of the little tables outside the cafe. The proprietor, on learning that Yeoman was a British pilot, refused to let him pay for the drinks.

Yeoman looked at Julia, almost as though he were seeing her for the first time. She looked tired. He reached over the table and patted her hand. 'I think you're bloody marvellous,' he said.

She smiled. 'Thanks. You're not so bad yourself. Sorry, but I was miles away just then, planning my next article. I'm a working girl, don't forget. You just wait until I write about your exploits; I'll turn you into a hero and embarrass the life out of you!'

He laughed and drained his glass, thinking suddenly of Wynne-Williams's escape story. 'There are others far more deserving of the adulation of the great American unwashed than me,' he said. He leaned towards her, his face becoming serious. 'Listen,' he told her, 'whatever you do, write the facts. Somebody's got to set the record straight. Somebody's got to tell the world about all the cock-ups, all the apathy, all the stupidity that helped to create this little lot. And somebody's got to tell the world, too, about all the beastliness and the bloody arrogance of people who think they can walk all over everybody else just because they've got a big stick.'

He sat back. 'I don't know whether I'll come through or not,' he continued. 'I just don't know. I've been in action for exactly a week, and already I've seen more than one man I was proud to call my friend get killed. I just thank God I'm not an infantryman; I don't think I could take that. But you'll come through all right, Julia; nothing is going to harm you. Look around you, at the heroism, the comradeship, the misery, the sheer bloody awfulness of it, and write about all these things. But leave glory out of it. My father went into the last war thinking there was glory in it, and came out of three years in the trenches hating the world. Yet even after that, people were still writing about glory. Don't you make that mistake. Not ever.'

He stopped suddenly and passed a hand wearily over his eyes. 'I'm sorry,' he apologized, 'I didn't mean to make a speech. God, I sound like a veteran, and I'm hardly dry behind the ears yet.'

She smiled. 'I understand, perhaps better than you think. I must admit that I feel a phoney at times, standing in the wings, so to speak, and watching somebody else's show. One thing I am certain about, though; the good guys are going to win in the end. No matter how black things may seem in Norway, or here, I can't see the British giving up without a hell of a fight. And I believe, although there are millions of folks back home who would shout me down for saying so, that America will make this her war too, before very long. And then the funny little man with the moustache had better watch out!'

She leaned back suddenly and sighed, tapping herself on the side of her head with her index finger. 'I must be crazy,' she said. 'We both must be crazy. Here we are with at least two whole hours to spend in gay Paree and what do we do? Sit around and talk about something we should both be doing our best to forget for a while. Come on, I'll give you a conducted tour. I know Paris like the back of my hand.'

They rode into the heart of the capital, with Julia giving a running commentary over Yeoman's shoulder.

'You should have seen this place a couple of months ago,' she yelled. 'I've always loved Paris in the springtime, with the chestnut trees bursting into leaf and the sun lighting up those gorgeous grey buildings. I used to spend hours standing in front of the shop windows of van Cleef,

Mauboussin and Cartier, just admiring the diamonds as the sun caught them. There were a few shortages. Some days you couldn't get sugar, or meat, and the patisseries were closed three days a week, but it never seemed to make much difference. Just before I left, on the second of May, there was a great party, a charity gala at the Marigny Theatre. Everybody was there, including your Duke of Windsor. I guess they don't have parties like that anymore.'

It came as a surprise to Yeoman to see queues in Paris. He had been familiar with the sight in England ever since the early days of the war, but somehow he had never associated the habit with anywhere else. He noticed that most of the queues were outside clothing and shoe shops. The Parisians, he thought, obviously get their priorities right, with food first on the agenda.

There was a marked increase in traffic as they approached the centre of Paris. In the Place de la Concorde, it was so dense that Yeoman was forced to stop. Most of the traffic here was military; Julia pointed out the Navy Ministry, outside which stood a convoy of lorries. Naval personnel swarmed like ants around them, loading what appeared to be files. 'The ship isn't even sinking yet,' Julia observed quietly, 'but it looks as though the rats are losing no time in getting out.'

'I'm famished,' Yeoman said. 'Let's grab something to eat.'

They found a café and sat down at a small marble-topped table under a striped awning, ordering rolls and coffee. Julia looked suddenly depressed. They sat in silence, watching the life of the city ebb and flow around them. 'I wouldn't have believed that a couple of weeks could have made so much difference,' Julia said. 'Everybody seems listless and resigned, as though they are meekly accepting the fact that the Germans will be here in a few days. They've just given up. And yet most of their armies are still intact.'

The flow of traffic built up gradually as they sat there, private cars laden with personal possessions crawling along nose to tail, heading south. A hundred yards up the road, outside what looked like a government building, a bonfire blazed on the pavement. Staff were running back and forth like ants, feeding the flames with documents. Charred scraps of paper floated through the air.

Yeoman looked at his watch. 'I think we ought to be going,' he said. 'I feel damned uncomfortable sitting here.'

They mounted the motor-bike and Yeoman eased his way through the crowded streets. Julia directed him across the square by the Hôtel de Ville to the Avenue Gabrielle, where the American Consulate stood. He pulled up a few yards from the main entrance. The Stars and Stripes flew bravely over the building, making a vivid splash of colour against the sky. It was a solid, reassuring sight, an island of sanity amid all the chaos.

They dismounted and stood on the pavement, facing one another. Julia reached out and took his hand.

'Well, George Yeoman, this is where we part company. Think you can find your way to the British Embassy all right?' He nodded.

'We won't say good-bye,' she smiled. 'I've a feeling London's my next port of call. Look me up there, if you get the chance.' She fished in her bag and produced a card. 'That's the address of the London office. It's in Holborn. But give me a couple of days' notice, if you can; you never know where I might be.'

Suddenly, her arms were around him and her cheek pressed against his. Then she was gone, running up the steps into the building, her parting words echoing behind her: 'Don't get yourself killed, George.'

He stood there for a long minute, staring at the empty doorway. There was a lump in his throat. He raised his hand and gently touched his cheek, remembering the softness of her skin against the bristles of his face. Julia.

Damn the war. Damn everything. He turned and swung a leg over the saddle, kicking the engine into bellowing life. He roared away up the avenue, seeing nothing but the stretch of road immediately in front of him, his mind a turmoil of painful emotions. Later, when he had time to think rationally, when life came to mean something more than the stink of petrol and cordite and the roar of a Rolls-Royce Merlin, he would analyse his feelings. And then, with all the clarity of his twenty years, he would know for certain that he was utterly, irrevocably, in love with Julia Connors.

*

The corridors of the British Embassy in the Faubourg St Honoré were thronged with people, both military and civilian. There was no panic here, but rather a sense of urgency, of tasks that needed to be carried out and little time in which to do them. Yeoman identified himself to an armed policeman at the door and was shown into the foyer, where a harassed clerk peered at him from behind a mound of papers on top of an enormous Victorian desk.

'Look, old chap,' the clerk fussed, 'I'm up to my neck in it. VIPs, and all that sort of thing. I'll sort you out in a minute. Have a seat over there, will you?'

Yeoman slumped into an armchair, feeling incredibly scruffy and out of place among the immaculate suits and uniforms that flowed past him. People stared at him curiously. Sardonically, he thought: maybe I ought to have a big placard on my chest proclaiming the fact that I'm a British pilot, in big red capitals. He hid his face in a two-month-old copy of *Punch*, and settled down to wait.

He must have dozed off. A sudden commotion awoke him. He looked around, blinking the sleep from his eyes. The foyer seemed to be full of diplomats and generals, all looking at their watches as though expecting something momentous to happen. It would really knock them for six, Yeoman thought, if Hitler appeared in the doorway. With sudden wild humour, he giggled uncontrollably. The group of diplomats nearest to him turned and glared. He returned to the sanctuary of *Punch*.

The clerk scurried over. 'Look here, old chap, I'm afraid we're going to have to shift you. We're expecting a VIP at any moment — a very, *very* important person, you understand. Can't have you flying types making the place untidy, what?'

The fruity voice of the man, who appeared more pretentious than any of the diplomats who were his superiors, was beginning to irritate Yeoman. He rose from his seat and mustered what he hoped was a fierce expression.

'No, old chap,' he said, emphasizing the words deliberately, '*you* look here. I was promised transport to take me to my squadron, and to my squadron I intend to go. So get your finger out, if you don't mind, or take me to somebody who can solve my particular problem.'

'All right, all right, old man, don't get het up.' The clerk looked uncomfortable. 'Fact is, it's not as simple as that. I'm afraid your squadron isn't there anymore. Not at Creil, I mean.'

Yeoman groaned, feeling his heart plummet into his boots. 'Then where the hell is it?' he demanded.

'Well, as far as we know they've gone up to Amiens. Something about providing air cover for the BEF. I'm really sorry about your position, but it's getting harder by the minute to get hold of any real information. Communications are falling apart. We tried to ring your Air Headquarters, but it seems to have vanished off the face of the earth. We don't really know what's going on up there.' The man looked a little hurt. 'You aren't the only one, you know. Everybody who's lost or strayed comes to us for help, and it's not nice to have to tell them we can't do much.'

Yeoman nodded, relaxing a little. 'All right, I'm sorry too, I didn't mean to be quite so abrupt. Any suggestions?'

The clerk shrugged. 'Well, all I can suggest is that you hang around for the time being. I'll keep on top of things for you as far as I can. We'll see if we can work something out. You've caught us at a bad moment, I'm afraid.'

Yeoman opened his mouth to speak, then closed it again as he noticed a general movement towards the door. He walked forward a few steps until he was standing beside a pillar, from where he could see across the foyer and past the groups of diplomats into the street.

Two limousines had drawn up outside. Men in uniform were milling around them, opening doors and saluting. The diplomats and army officers formed two lanes in the foyer. The clerk kept trying to push Yeoman into the shadows but he resisted, his curiosity getting the upper hand.

A figure emerged from the second limousine: the figure of a burly man, wearing a dark suit and hat, the stub of a cigar thrust into the corner of his mouth. He shook hands with someone who must have been the ambassador and a couple of others, then stumped up the steps towards the main door, looking neither to left nor right. He was followed by a very tall officer, a craggy-faced man who walked with a slight stoop. He wore a lot of medal ribbons, and the red tabs of a general.

Yeoman had eyes only for the burly man who stalked into the embassy, nodding curtly to the waiting diplomats. His whole body exuded defiance, dedication and purpose.

So this is what he looks like in the flesh, the pilot thought. The man who had taken over the reins of power from the weary, disillusioned Neville Chamber-lain; the man on whose leadership and unswerving purpose the hopes of the British people were now pinned. Winston Churchill.

He felt something akin to panic as Churchill looked straight in his direction. If there had been a hole handy, Yeoman would have crawled into it. He wished he had followed the clerk's advice and got out of the way. All heads turned towards him. He had never felt so conspicuous.

Without altering his pace, the Prime Minister turned sharply left and barged his way through the line of diplomats, bearing down on the pilot, head lowered like a charging bull. Out of the corner of his eye, Yeoman saw the clerk making himself scarce.

Churchill stumped to a halt and removed the cigar stub from his lips, scowling at the pilot. He eyed Yeoman up and down.

'Well, young man,' he growled. 'It would appear from your attire that you are some sort of aviator. Pray give an account of yourself.'

Yeoman swallowed hard and briefly recounted his adventures since the attack on the Meuse bridges. When he had finished, the Prime Minister, who had listened throughout in silence, grunted and raised an eyebrow.

'So. And in the course of your actions, did you succeed in destroying any German machines?'

'Three, sir. A Dornier and two Messerschmitts.'

Churchill nodded. 'And now I am to understand that you wish to rejoin your unit at the earliest possible moment?'

'Yes, sir, but there are snags. I was originally told that my squadron was at Creil, not far from here, but now I am informed that it has moved to Amiens. I don't know how I am going to get there. I've travelled over half of France already.'

The Prime Minister looked away, apparently lost in thought. Then, to Yeoman's intense surprise, he smiled. 'Young man,' he said, 'it is my privilege to shake you by the hand. I thank providence for you, and those like you. I think I may be able to assist you.'

He turned and spoke rapidly to the tall general. Yeoman couldn't catch more than the odd word. The general looked at the pilot, his cold, bright eyes boring into him, and nodded.

'Young man,' Churchill said, turning back to him, 'you will have to suffer another small delay which will not, I trust, exceed forty-five minutes. Then you will be collected and seen on your way. Good-bye, and good luck.'

Yeoman began to stammer his thanks, but Churchill cut him short with a wave of his hand. The pilot watched his retreating back as he plodded away, followed by his entourage.

Much later, he learned that the Prime Minister had flown to Paris for urgent consultations with Paul Reynaud, France's Premier, and General Gamelin, the French C-in-C; consultations which were to have no small influence on the eventual outcome of the Battle of France. Yeoman was to marvel that Churchill, with such weighty matters on his mind, should have found time to deal with the plight of a humble sergeant pilot. He was conscious that he had shaken hands with a very great man, and began to understand that a man's greatness lay not only in the achievement of momentous things, but also in the consideration and understanding of all those lesser beings with whom he came into contact.

Yeoman had a sudden thought. He went and found the clerk and asked him to look after the motor-cycle, giving him the address of the inn at Ecury. The man promised to see that the bike was carefully stored away, and the pilot's conscience felt easier as he settled down to wait.

Churchill proved to be as good as his word. After just over half an hour, the tall general strode through the foyer, followed by three staff1 officers. One of them beckoned Yeoman to follow. They went outside to one of the waiting limousines; the three officers climbed into the back and Yeoman sat next to the driver, a stony-faced civilian who said not a word.

The car moved smoothly through the city, heading north. The driver obviously knew his business, threading his way through a maze of side streets to avoid the main mass of traffic. Yeoman had no idea where they were going, but at least it was in the right direction.

The built-up areas fell behind, and the traffic became less dense. The exodus from Paris was towards the south, away from the German threat. After a few more minutes, Yeoman looked ahead with sudden interest as an airfield appeared on the left-hand side of the road. The driver turned in at the main gate and stopped at a striped barrier. Beside it, a wooden sign proclaimed: Aéroport du Bourget.

Two gendarmes approached the car and checked the passes of the driver and the three officers. One of the latter, who spoke fluent French, must have explained Yeoman's presence, because one of the gendarmes eyed him briefly and then nodded, apparently satisfied. The barrier was raised and the car purred on, heading for a cluster of buildings on the far side of the airfield.

A few aircraft stood in front of the hangars. One of them, a gleaming twin-engined machine, puzzled the pilot for a few moments until he recalled a photograph he had seen in *Flight*. It was a de Havilland Flamingo airliner, one of a trio which the RAF had pressed into service on the outbreak of war as VIP transports. It must, he thought, be the machine which had brought Churchill to Paris. His belief was confirmed by the presence, close by, of two sleek fighters. They were Spitfires, the first he had seen in France. They must have been detailed to escort the airliner.

The car cruised on past a handful of French transport and communications aircraft and stopped at the end of the line beside a twin-engined biplane that bore RAF camouflage and markings. Yeoman identified it as a de Havilland Dragon Rapide; he knew that an RAF squadron, No. 81, used the machines for communications and light transport duties.

An army corporal came running up and opened the rear door. The staff officers climbed out, the tall general returning the NCO's salute. Yeoman got out too, wondering what to do. The general called him over. He towered a good head and shoulders above the pilot.

'Sergeant,' he said, 'we are flying north to Norrent-Fontès. We propose to land at Amiens to disembark you. We shall be taking off in ten minutes. I suggest you report to the pilot of the aircraft.'

Yeoman thanked him, came briefly to attention and walked over to the Rapide, poking his head through the door. There was no one about. He climbed inside and walked up the aisle between the seats, noting the carpeting and curtains that adorned the interior of the machine. Some people, he thought, certainly travel in style.

He entered the cockpit and sat down in the right-hand seat, looking over the unfamiliar layout. The Rapide's nose was well forward of the wings and the view was excellent.

'Hello! What are you doing in my aeroplane?'

Yeoman jumped, startled by the sudden voice. He started to get up as an RAF officer, a squadron leader, squeezed through the hatch behind him. The newcomer told him to stay where he was, and settled himself in the seat opposite.

'You're Sergeant Yeoman, I presume. I've just heard about you. Well, Yeoman, you're a bit of a bloody nuisance, but we'll do our best to get you where you want to be. My name's Matthews.' He turned and grinned at the young pilot. Yeoman noticed his grey hair, and the two rows of medal ribbons on his tunic. One of them was the Distinguished Service Order. Once again, his curiosity got the better of him.

'Were you a pilot in the last war, sir?' he asked. Matthews nodded.

'It makes me feel really old when somebody asks that question,' he grinned, 'but I'm afraid I can't deny it. I flew DH 9s with Trenchard's bombing force in 1918, then went out to North Russia in '19 with the Allied Intervention Force. That's where I first came across the general.' He jerked a thumb towards the passenger cabin.

'The general?' Yeoman asked.

'Yes, General Ironside. Didn't you know that's who he is? Chief of the Imperial General Staff, no less. You're in exalted company, son. He commanded the Murmansk-Archangel front during the Intervention, and a damn' fine soldier he was, too.'

We're going to need a few like that to pull us out of this mess, Yeoman thought, although he didn't voice his opinion. Matthews was, after all, a senior officer.

Matthews busied himself with the starting checks and then motioned through the side window to an airman, who made sure the chocks were in position. The Rapide's Gypsy engines started effortlessly; Matthews looked back into the cabin, making sure that his passengers were strapped in, and then signalled for the chocks to be pulled away.

Matthews taxied out and turned the Rapide into wind, opening the throttles. The tail came up quickly and the biplane lifted cleanly into the air, settling down into a steady climb. Matthews took her up to four thousand feet. Yeoman noted the heading: 358 degrees magnetic. The Rapide laboured along at a hundred miles an hour.

Yeoman asked the pilot if he had heard the latest news from the front. Matthews's face became serious.

'It's not so good, I'm afraid,' he told the younger man. 'The Huns have broken through on the Meuse front, but I dare say you know all about that already. They've dropped paratroops all over Holland and their armour is knocking hell out of the Belgian Army. I flew up to Liège yesterday; the BEF were moving up to the Dyle, but they hadn't made any serious contact by the time I left. I expect the picture's changed by now, though.'

The flight to Amiens lasted forty minutes. As the Rapide touched down, Yeoman saw that the airfield was stiff with British and French aircraft; there were Battles, Blenheims and Hurricanes everywhere, intermingled with French Moranes and Curtiss Hawks.

The Rapide stopped outside the airfield buildings. Yeoman took his leave of Matthews and went back through the cabin, pausing to thank Ironside. The general nodded and wished him good luck. Yeoman opened the door and jumped down on to the grass, narrowing his eyes as the slipstream from the Rapide's port propeller caught him. He made sure the door was shut, then ducked away past the wingtip, giving the thumbs-up to Matthews. The pilot waved back and the Rapide moved forward. Yeoman watched it as it took off and dwindled in the evening sky. It looked completely out of place in comparison with the angular lines of the warplanes, like a stately old maid who had somehow stumbled on a nest of pirates.

Yeoman turned and walked towards the buildings. A wing commander emerged from a doorway, carrying a parachute. Yeoman approached him.

'Excuse me, sir. I'm Sergeant Yeoman, 505 Squadron. I'm reporting back after being shot down and I'm looking for my unit. I'm told they're here.'

The wing commander looked puzzled for a moment, then his face brightened. 'Oh, yes, the new arrivals. They're over there, I think.' He indicated a cluster of tents half a mile away, on the other side of the airfield. Yeoman made out the camouflaged outlines of Hurricanes, parked nearby. He thanked the wing commander and started walking.

The squadron was obviously on readiness. The pilots were lounging beside their aircraft. As he drew nearer, Yeoman felt a great upsurge of joy as he picked out the faces that had become so familiar to him in just a few short days. Jim Callender got up, grinning, and slapped him on the back. 'Just look at it! Living proof that only the good die young!'

Wynne-Williams's moustache twitched. 'Come on, George, have some tea and tell us what happened to you. You look as though you've been shooting bears and raping virgins, or rather the other way round.'

'If I tell you,' Yeoman said, falling gratefully into a deck-chair, 'you won't believe me.'

He was right.

# CHAPTER TEN

Twenty-nine thousand feet below, the Channel sparkled in the morning sun. Visibility was perfect, with both the French and British coasts clearly visible. Dungeness was dead ahead. It was a beautiful panorama.

Yeoman was in no mood to enjoy it. He was frozen stiff, and having trouble with icing. The windscreen was opaque, making it hard to see Wynne-Williams's Hurricane, a few hundred yards ahead and to the right, and harder still to see their quarry; a high-flying Dornier 17, three miles in front of them and still a thousand feet higher, streaming a long, arrow-straight condensation trail.

It was the morning of 19 May. Yeoman had not flown since his return to the squadron, partly because the MO had forbidden it, and partly because the squadron had pulled back to Calais on the eighteenth. The picture of air strength at Amiens, Yeoman had soon discovered, had been an illusion; the Blenheims had belonged to two squadrons of No. 2 Group, based in England, and they had landed at Amiens to refuel before attacking enemy columns in Belgium. They had been shot to pieces.

The Allied situation had changed dramatically for the worse over the past forty-eight hours. By 18 May, with two German armoured divisions sweeping down on Arras, it had become clear that the British Expeditionary Force could not stem the enemy advance through Belgium. The Belgian and French Armies were collapsing on either flank, and the BEF would have its work cut out to extricate itself from the trap that threatened to close around it.

On the eighteenth, Lord Gort, the BEF's commander, had ordered the evacuation to begin of wounded and non-combatant personnel from three main ports: Boulogne, Calais and Dunkirk. Since it was expected that the Luftwaffe would try to interfere with the evacuations, 505 Squadron had been detailed to provide air cover over Calais and Boulogne. Farther up the coast, at Dunkirk, patrols would be carried out by the Spitfire and Hurricane squadrons of Fighter Command's No. 11 Group, based in the south-east of England.

Yeoman and Wynne-Williams had been on readiness that morning, spending an uncomfortable hour strapped into their Hurricanes. It had been a relief when, at nine o'clock, they had taken off in response to a sudden alert, climbing hard over Calais. They had circled the port several times at eighteen thousand feet before they sighted the slender contrail, crossing the coast a few miles to the north.

The Dornier was fast. The two Hurricanes managed to close the distance a little, but then the German pilot poured on the coals and maintained his lead. Yeoman swore fluently to himself as the altimeter wavered around the 29,000-foot mark and refused to climb any higher. The performance of Wynne-Williams's fighter was better, and it gradually began to draw away.

In the distance, the Dornier's contrail described a curve in the sky as the reconnaissance aircraft crossed the English coast near Dungeness and turned northeastwards, its mission apparently to photograph the coastal airfields as far as Manston. Wynne-Williams's voice came over the radio.

'George, we've got him. The bugger's got to go home sometime. We'll fly parallel to him for a bit.'

The two Hurricanes turned up the Channel, keeping the coast on their port wingtips. The Dornier's contrail crawled over Folkestone. Suddenly, it kinked sharply as the German pilot steep-turned. A few moments later it vanished. Two more trails appeared briefly like thin slashes of chalk, some distance away from the Dornier, then they too disappeared. No. 11 Group's fighters, probably Spitfires at that height, were hot on the German's tail and he was losing no time in getting clear.

'Damn it, I've lost him. Keep your eyes peeled, George, he'll be diving like hell.'

Yeoman was the first to locate the Dornier again, its cruciform shape showing up darkly against the glittering surface of the sea. It was already several thousand feet lower than the Hurricanes and was crossing underneath them to their left. There was no sign of the fighters that were supposedly chasing it.

Wynne-Williams winged over and dived in pursuit, followed by Yeoman. The Dornier was still diving, its pilot intent on getting down to wave-top height to prevent attacks from underneath. Yeoman was astonished by the bomber's speed; the Hurricanes were doing four hundred miles per hour and more in the dive, but were closing with the Dornier painfully slowly. Perhaps the aircraft had been stripped of a lot of equipment to enable it to carry out its high-flying missions more effectively.

The Dornier levelled out at five hundred feet and sped towards Cap Gris Nez, followed by the Hurricanes. Yeoman's aircraft creaked and groaned alarmingly as it came out of its headlong plunge. The pilot felt slightly dizzy as the sea blurred under him, the wave-crests flashing past. A few moments earlier the Channel had looked like a glassy sheet, silent and peaceful; now it appeared angry and forbidding, as though ready to pluck the fleeting aircraft from the sky.

The Dornier was gradually creeping towards them. Wynne-Williams was two hundred yards ahead of Yeoman, and the latter saw his Hurricane shudder as he opened fire at extreme range. The burst kicked up spray slightly to the left of the bomber. Wynne-Williams fired again. It was either a tremendous fluke, or a very expert piece of shooting. Smoke poured back from the Dornier's port engine and the aircraft climbed steeply, losing speed rapidly. Wynne-Williams corrected his aim and fired again, chopping at the Dornier in short, deadly bursts. With both engines now on fire the bomber levelled out and twisted away across the sea, the pilot desperately trying to gain the coast. A parachute broke away, a thin yellow streamer with a shapeless bundle attached to it. It was swallowed up by the waves before it had a chance to deploy.

The Dornier faltered and went into a descending turn to the right. It was finished, and Wynne-Williams knew it. He drew off to one side. Yeoman watched, fascinated, imagining the agony of the German pilot as he struggled in vain to control the dying aircraft. Yeoman had been an interested spectator throughout; it had been entirely Wynne-Williams's show.

The Dornier's wingtip hit the water. A plume of spray shimmered in the sunlight. The next instant the bomber was gone. Wynne-Williams flew low over the spot and Yeoman followed him, looking down. The Dornier's grave was marked by a spreading patch of oil and a few islands of wreckage, bobbing on the surface of the Channel.

Yeoman jumped as a shadow flashed suddenly across his cockpit. He looked up, startled, then relaxed. Sitting a few feet away from his wingtip was the slender, shark-like shape of a Spitfire, presumably one of the aircraft that had been chasing the Dornier. The Spit's pilot, in a gesture of supreme disgust at being robbed of his prey, stuck two fingers up at Yeoman, then stood his fighter on its wingtip and curved gracefully away towards the English coast. Yeoman watched it go, admiring the Spitfire's slender fuselage and elliptical wings. He wondered if he would ever get his hands on one.

'Come on, George, let's go home.'

Yeoman formed up alongside Wynne-Williams and the two Hurricanes set course for Calais, the pilots leaning out their fuel mixture as far as they dared. The chase had used up a lot of petrol. They landed at Calais-Marck airfield with only a couple of gallons to spare.

By noon on 19 May, the Luftwaffe had become undisputed mistress of the sky over the battlefront. The battered remnants of the British Air Forces in France were regrouping on the Cherbourg peninsula, and apart from the depleted Hurricane squadrons were able to take no further part in the battle for the time being. The French, too, with much of their fighter and bomber strength wiped out on the ground, were utterly disorganized, and making desperate attempts to regroup south of the river Somme.

The German armour was on the advance everywhere, supported by the fearful combination of Henschel spotter aircraft and Stuka dive-bombers. On 18 May, one of the few determined French armoured counterattacks — by the 4th Division Cuirassée at Montcornet — had been shattered by Stukas almost before it had had time to get under way. It was a bitter blow for the French division's commander, a young colonel whose repeated requests for French spotter aircraft to work together with tanks had been ignored by the High Command. His name was Charles de Gaulle.

In the north the Germans were gathering their resources for the big push designed to split the Allied armies in two and take the Panzer spearhead to the Channel coast. While Erwin Rommel's armoured division prepared to by-pass Arras and encircle the British forces there — the Germans unaware that the British armour would soon give them a bloody nose and check their onrush for a short time — General Heinz Guderian's Panzer Corps massed on a line between Cambrai and Péronne, ready to sweep down and capture Arras before thrusting on to reach the sea at Abbeville, on the Somme estuary.

On the afternoon of the nineteenth, small groups of high-flying German bombers began the Luftwaffe's air offensive against Boulogne and Calais. The first attack, at two o'clock, took 505 Squadron completely by surprise. Taking advantage of scattered cloud cover, twelve Heinkels slipped over the top of Calais-Marck at fifteen thousand feet. While ten of them headed for the port, the other two turned and flew back over the airfield, unloading their bombs just as the pilots raced for their Hurricanes.

Yeoman, whose Hurricane was in the process of being rearmed, heard the strange rustling noise of the falling bombs and threw himself down, hugging the grass, as the rustle swelled to an ear-piercing shriek. He never heard the explosions, but the ground heaved under him and the concussion struck him like a hammer-blow, jarring him from head to foot. Pebbles and clods of earth rained around him.

He raised his head and looked around cautiously. A great cloud of dust and smoke hung over the centre of the airfield, across which the bombs had fallen, apparently without doing any real damage. He picked himself up stiffly and watched as two sections of Hurricanes raced through the smoke, the pilots tucking up their wheels as soon as they were airborne and climbing hard towards the coast, over which the German formation was turning at the end of its bombing run. He saw three or four columns of smoke shoot up from Calais, and a few moments later the boom of the explosions reached him.

The second stick of bombs aimed at the airfield had fallen outside the perimeter, exploding among the white-painted houses of a small hamlet that lay half a mile from the outskirts of the village of Marck. Smoke and flames rose from it.

Others had seen the tragedy, too, and figures ran towards the Morris truck that stood outside the operations hut, bent on getting over there as quickly as possible to give what help they could. Yeoman was the first to reach the vehicle, and jumped into the driving seat. Half a dozen airmen climbed into the back. The passenger door opened and the squadron adjutant, Flight-Lieutenant King, scrambled in with difficulty. A much-decorated First World War pilot, he had an artificial leg, yet despite the handicap, he could move with surprising agility.

The others clung on grimly as Yeoman sent the truck bouncing at speed round the perimeter, heading for a gap in the hedge that bordered the Marck road. It took him less than five minutes to reach the hamlet. A heap of fallen rubble barred the vehicle's path as it came to the outskirts, forcing Yeoman to pull up by the roadside.

They jumped down and clawed their way over the shattered masonry, coughing in the clouds of dust that still hung in the air. On the other side, the dust and smoke pall was so dense that it was difficult to see anything at all.

The RAF men moved slowly forward into the murk, King limping along a few yards in the rear. Suddenly, they stopped dead.

Ahead of them, a figure emerged from the smoke. It was an elderly woman. Her clothing hung in rags and blood streamed down her face from a dozen cuts. She stumbled past the horrified airmen, her eyes glazed and stunned. Yeoman stretched out a hand to her, but he might just as well not have existed. The woman blundered into a fragment of wall and stopped dead, feeling the rough stone with her bloodstained hands. Then she sank down at its foot, an inert and pathetic bundle. King limped over to her, unfastening the first-aid pack he carried. Yeoman and the others turned and plunged into the acrid smoke.

The stick of bombs appeared to have fallen diagonally across the hamlet.

The whole place was in ruins. Some of the inhabitants, dazed with shock and horror, were clawing at shattered stonework and beams where picturesque houses had once stood.

A young man stood beside a pile of rubble, tears washing rivulets through the grime that caked his distraught face. 'Aidez-moi!' he cried, as the airmen ran towards him. 'Pour l'amour de Dieu, aidez-moi! Ma femme ... mes enfants ...' he broke off and buried his face in his hands, weeping. Yeoman shook him roughly by the shoulder. 'Come on,' he yelled, 'dig! Get to work!'

They tore their hands bloody, burrowing a pathway into the wrecked cottage. Yeoman lost all count of time as he worked, coughing frequently to clear the dust from his clogged throat.

His hand touched something soft, and he recoiled instinctively. Carefully, he brushed away a layer of dust and grit, exposing a woman's face. Her forehead was crushed and she was clearly dead. The Frenchman screamed and hurled himself forward, clutching at the debris that pinned down the body. Yeoman tried to pull him away. The man, crazed with horror and grief, picked up a piece of stone and rounded on the pilot, his arm raised to strike. Yeoman took a deep breath and hit him on the point of the jaw, as hard as he could. The man subsided.

'Poor bastard,' one of the airmen muttered.

Yeoman held up his hand for silence. A thin wail, like that of a kitten in distress, came from the midst of the rubble. They listened intently, and heard it again. This time, there was no mistaking the whimper of a terrified child.

They worked on, joined now by some villagers, lifting away blocks of stone. The woman's body was removed and covered with a blanket. Yeoman, lying on his stomach in a tunnel of fallen beams, urged himself on relentlessly as the child's cry came once more, closer now. His way was barred by a large block of stone. He managed to get his hands round it, and shouted to the helpers to pull him out by the legs. They dragged him from the tunnel inch by inch, block and all, pieces of sharp stone and splintered glass tearing his uniform to shreds and lacerating his skin.

At last he was free. He shoved the stone block to one side, took a few gulps of air and plunged back into the tunnel again, worming his way towards the cavity where the big stone had been. He found himself looking into the remains of what had apparently been a kitchen. Gradually, as his eyes got accustomed to the gloom, he began to pick out details; smashed furniture, broken pots, scattered pans — and, in the centre, a large table, like an island amid the sea of devastation.

Underneath it, like wild animals in a cave, two small boys cowered in terror, their faces pale in the semidarkness. They were perhaps eight or nine years old, and looked like twins. The pilot spoke to them, and they cowered back even farther into their cavern.

Yeoman went on talking, trying to keep his voice soft and finding it hard because of the grit that caked his throat. The children clearly didn't understand a word he said, but he kept on talking, using the tones he would have used to soothe a fearful, quivering pup. He could not squeeze into what was left of the kitchen, because the hole was too narrow and any attempt to move more rubble might cause the whole lot to collapse. The children would have to come to him.

After a while, his voice seemed to have the desired effect. Slowly, one of the children crawled out from under the table and came towards him. Yeoman reached out and took the child's hand in his, squeezing it reassuringly. He pulled the child towards him and managed to get a firm grip under his armpits. Then, hoarsely, he called to the helpers to pull them both out.

A few minutes later both boys were weeping in their father's arms, one of the airmen having gone in to retrieve the second child. The Frenchman was calmer now, and pathetically grateful that his children were safe.

Help had arrived quickly from Marck, and by this time rescue teams were at work among the other shattered houses, lifting the dead and the half-dead from the rubble. Ten civilians had died, half of them children.

There was nothing more for the airmen to do. They went back to their truck and returned to the airfield. King took the wheel; the flesh of Yeoman's palms was badly torn, turning both hands into savage pools of pain.

The Hurricanes were back. They had shot down two of the Heinkels and damaged a third. Flight-Lieutenant Rogerson had been slightly wounded in the leg by a 7.7-mm bullet. Yeoman went off to see the MO, who cleaned up his hands, smeared them with ointment and bandaged them. Yeoman flexed his fingers painfully; at least, he thought, he would still be able to handle the controls of his fighter.

Some time later, a Dornier reconnaissance aircraft flew high over the area. Luftwaffe intelligence officers pored over the photographs it brought back to base, and made their report.

'Raid 112, 14.10 hours, 19 May 1940. Target: Calais. Bombing altitude: 3500 metres. Visibility: good. Photographic results: good.

'Observation: Some damage caused to the port installations and Fort Lapin. One substantial fire still burning in the port area, time 16.00 hours. One stick of bombs plotted running NE/SW across Calais-Marck airfield. No significant damage. Second stick of bombs plotted running NE/SW just outside airfield perimeter. Apparent damage to group of buildings, which may or may not have military significance.'

\*

The German bombers returned to Calais early that evening, and this time the Hurricanes of 505 Squadron were ready for them. The squadron had managed to put up two and a half sections — in other words eight Hurricanes. They were stepped up over the port between fifteen and twenty thousand feet, with Hillier's Red Section at the lowest level. Next came Yellow Section, led by Rogerson, and right on top were the two fighters of Blue Section — Yeoman and Wynne-Williams. Yeoman's hands smarted like hell and, deep down, he would have welcomed the chance to stay on the ground, but there had been no reserve pilot — and, he reflected, if Rogerson could put up with his injured leg, he, Yeoman, could tolerate a few scratches.

The Germans came out of the east, heading arrow-straight for Calais like menacing birds of prey. There were twenty-four of them; Junkers 87 Stukas, flying in three beautiful echelons at twelve thousand feet.

The Hurricane pilots searched the sky carefully. There appeared to be no fighter escort. It was too good to be true. The British pilots had all the advantages, including height and sun.

Hillier's voice crackled over the radio. 'Squadron, Sections astern, attack!' Yeoman saw Red and Yellow Sections go into a long, shallow dive towards the enemy, who were still some five miles away from Calais. A moment later he and Wynne-Williams followed suit, heading for the rearmost of the German echelons.

The three Hurricanes of Red Section fanned out, the pilots selecting their individual targets and attacking head-on. Yeoman saw Hillier open fire and a Stuka blow up with a terrific explosion, scattering burning wreckage. Another Stuka on its right faltered and dropped out of formation, crippled by the blast. Then there was no time to see anything else except his own target, the Stuka on the extreme left of the third echelon.

The pain in his hands was forgotten and a savage exultation welled up inside him as the Junkers leaped to meet him. The German's yellow-painted spinner crept into his sight and his thumb jabbed down on the firing-button, loosing off a two-second burst that raked the enemy aircraft from nose to tail. He caught a fleeting glimpse of the long glasshouse cockpit shattering into fragments, and then he was streaking over the Stuka like a flash of lightning.

He pulled up hard and stall-turned, arrowing down to attack from astern. His Stuka, its pilot probably dead at the controls, was fluttering earthwards like a falling leaf. A second dive-bomber, Wynne-Williams's victim, was also plunging down, spewing white flames.

Yeoman selected another target, a Stuka that was steep-turning ahead of him. He followed it in the turn, ignoring the tracer that arc'd towards him from its rear gunner. For the first time in air combat, with a shock that was naked and physical, he felt a burning, murderous anger against the men he was going to kill. He wanted to kill them, to strew their charred fragments over the French countryside. Bastards, he thought, and pressed the gun-button again, literally chopping the Stuka to pieces from a range of a hundred yards. Fire. For Chantal and little Etienne, lying bloodstained on a dusty French road. Fire. For Celine, the little girl who no longer had a mother. Fire. For the young man in the village who no longer had a wife. Bastards!

The rear gunner was dead, a bloodstained bundle sprawled over his gun. The Stuka was in shreds. Flames licked back from its engine. The front section of its canopy flew off and whirled away in the slipstream. The dive-bomber lost speed. Yeoman saw the pilot trying to struggle clear.

Yeoman throttled back. He raised the Hurricane's nose a little. Then, quite deliberately, he blew the enemy pilot apart with a short, savage burst of fire.

The doomed Stuka curved over on its back and went down. Yeoman pulled away. He was sweating and trembling. The pain came back into his hands. Blood was soaking through the bandages.

He looked around. There seemed to be Hurricanes everywhere, buzzing like angry wasps on a window pane. Columns of smoke, like tombstones, marked the graves of a dozen Stukas. The remainder had dropped their bombs and fled, harried by more fighters. Yeoman was puzzled for a moment; there weren't that many Hurricanes. Then he saw that the fighters were French Moranes, which had come up from the south at the last moment and hurled themselves into the fray.

It had been a massacre. When the pilots of 505 Squadron landed and counted the score, they found that they had destroyed eleven Stukas for certain. The French pilots had accounted for four more. No bombs had fallen on Calais. It was the last time that the hated dive-bombers would venture into defended air-space without strong fighter cover.

It was also 505 Squadron's last combat while flying from the soil of France. That night, the pilots received orders to pack everything they could and fly their surviving Hurricanes to Manston the following morning. A Bristol Bombay transport arrived to ferry out the rest. The news was received with mixed feelings, which Callender summed up: 'Why? Now when we feel we're getting the upper hand? Why the hell don't they send us more fighters? We can beat hell out of the Luftwaffe, we all know we can. If only we had more Hurricanes!'

There was one bright spot in the atmosphere of general gloom. Just after dark Henry turned up, still driving the Fordson tender. It was riddled with holes; he had been strafed for most of the way from Châlons. Henry was unscathed, but the signals corporal with him had a nasty shoulder wound and kept passing out. He was whipped off to hospital in Calais.

The squadron took off for Manston on schedule, leaving Calais-Marck deserted apart from a demolition team. They were to blow up the installations and fuel dump before embarking at the port.

That same day, General Guderian's Panzer Corps reached the Channel coast at Abbeville and raced on for a further twenty miles up the coast, slicing through a British infantry brigade, before poising for an all-out assault on Boulogne and Calais. Farther north, in Flanders, the bulk of the British Expeditionary Force, its position no longer tenable, was already beginning its gallant fighting retreat towards the port of Dunkirk.

## CHAPTER ELEVEN

The thing that Yeoman would always remember best about the squadron's return to England was the cleanliness: the luxury of a hot bath, the crispness of clean sheets, the shedding of clothing which he had worn almost continuously for ten days. He slept for the best part of twenty-four hours; they all did, and they all awoke feeling terrible. It would take more than a few hours' sleep, induced with the help of pills, to remove the tautness from their overstretched nerves.

Some of the AASF's Hurricane squadrons, they learned, had remained in France, operating for as long as they could from bases south of the Somme, pitifully lacking in spare parts and replacement aircraft. From now on, cover for the retreating Allied forces would be provided exclusively by the home-based squadrons of RAF Fighter Command.

On 21 May, having turned over their surviving Hurricanes to the aircraft pool at Manston, the personnel of 505 Squadron entrained for Church Fenton, in Yorkshire, to rest and reform. A week later, up to full strength once more, they were on their way back to Kent, and the war. It had been a hectic seven days, and any hope Yeoman had entertained of visiting his father had been quickly dashed. He had managed to write, though, almost every night before he collapsed dog-tired into bed; at least the old man knew that he was safe.

During that week, events across the Channel moved inexorably towards their momentous climax. On 25 May Boulogne fell, and the next day the haggard defenders of Calais, starved of ammunition and supplies, bombed incessantly by Stukas, surrendered to the 10th Panzer Division and marched into captivity.

This time, the Stukas had come with an umbrella of Messerschmitts. Fighter Wing 66 was there, and for Joachim Richter the morning of 26 May was a memorable occasion; his first encounter with Spitfires. It had not been a pleasant experience.

It happened at nine o'clock, as wave after wave of dive-bombers pounded the Citadel Fortress, the last bastion in Calais. Sixty

Messerschmitts were escorting them, stepped up to twenty thousand feet, glittering in the morning sun.

The 109s circled watchfully over the port as the Stukas peeled off, flight after flight plunging down towards their objective. Within minutes, a great pall of dust and smoke hung over the Citadel and the harbour. Underneath the holocaust, Allied ships continued their work of evacuation, trailing their arrow-heads of foam out to the sanctuary of the sea. From his vantage point high above, Richter saw a flight of Stukas dive on them, spearing down through the black blotches of the antiaircraft fire. A Junkers was hit and dissolved in an orange ball of flame, rolling slowly over and over until it was extinguished by the waves. The remainder pressed home their attack and a warship, probably a destroyer, disintegrated in a great, slow explosion. Richter watched in horrified fascination as a boiling mushroom of flame and smoke billowed upwards. Debris cascaded into the water in a spreading circle of white foam. When the smoke cleared, Richter saw that the warship had turned turtle. A moment later, it slid beneath the surface.

Suddenly, shouts of alarm echoed over the radio. Enemy fighters were coming in, speeding like arrows across the Channel. Richter's flight swung out over the coast, and a few moments later the young pilot spotted the enemy, flying at about fifteen thousand feet. As he watched, six of them broke away and streaked towards the dive-bombers; the other six climbed hard to take on the escorting Messerschmitts.

Richter had time to marvel at the courage of the British pilots, taking on such overwhelming odds without hesitation, before his flight went diving to meet the Spitfires head-on.

The Spitfires were fast, faster than either the Hurricanes or the Moranes he had encountered in action so far. Within seconds, they had swelled from tiny dots to full-size aircraft, converging on the Messerschmitts at a closing speed of over six hundred miles per hour, firing as they came. Richter flinched as a Spitfire loomed in his windshield, the leading edges of its wings lit up by the flashes of its eight machine-guns. He held his course grimly, returning the fire. There was a sudden almighty bang and the top left-hand corner of his armoured windscreen starred as a .303 bullet struck it.

Both pilots lost their nerve at the same instant and broke hard, fortunately in opposite directions. Richter kept on turning, craning his neck and swearing as he lost sight of the other aircraft. Another Spitfire flashed overhead, the roundels on its wings glaring like eyes. Yet another fleeted across his nose and he fired, missing hopelessly.

An aircraft fell past, staining the sky with a twisting spiral of smoke. Impossible to tell whether it was friend or foe.

He turned in the opposite direction and looked around. Suddenly, there was a flash and a bang as bullets hammered into the Emil's port wing. The fighter shuddered. Before Richter had time to react, a shadow blotted out the sun. He looked up, startled, his heart lurching. A few feet above his face was the pale blue belly of a Spitfire, streaked with oil and grime. His attacker had made a critical mistake, misjudging the Messerschmitt's speed and overshooting. Richter jerked up the nose of his fighter, loosing off a burst as the Spitfire passed him. He saw a flash as one of his shells found its mark in the enemy's rear fuselage.

The Spitfire pulled round in a tight turn. Richter followed him, hauling the Messerschmitt round. It was no use. Gradually, the Spitfire edged away from his sights. Another few moments and the bastard would be on his tail, and the hunter would become the hunted. Those Spitfires could certainly turn! He wondered if the Tommy was faster than the Emil in a dive. He hoped not. It might be his only chance of escaping if things got too hot.

Suddenly, inexplicably, the Spitfire rolled out of its turn. Its nose went down and it headed for the sea in a shallow dive. Richter went after him at full throttle, the engine screaming and the Emil's wings quivering and vibrating. He glanced quickly at the bullet holes stitched across the port wing, but the damage did not seem too serious. Nevertheless, he would need to be careful.

He made a slight adjustment to his sights and opened fire. His tracers fell away well below the target. He closed the radiator cooling flaps, risking the possibility of his engine overheating in exchange for reducing the drag a little and gaining a few more miles per hour.

The dive became steeper. Richter's eardrums popped furiously and his head pounded. The airspeed indicator registered over four hundred miles per hour and the temperature gauge was climbing rapidly. The engine was on the point of boiling. If he was going to get his Tommy, it had to be soon.

The distance between the two aircraft narrowed slowly. They were down to six thousand feet, and already well out over the Channel. Richter fired at extreme range, almost refusing to believe his eyes as he saw his tracers disappearing into the Spitfire's fuselage, just aft of the cockpit.

The Spitfire began to twist and turn in a frantic attempt to escape. Richter kept after him, throttle wide open, firing in two-second bursts. A thin smoke-trail began to stream out behind the Spitfire and it went into a sudden climb. Its cockpit canopy flew off and the pilot baled out, a dark bundle tumbling over and over towards the sea. The Spitfire continued its upwards trajectory for a few hundred feet, then stalled and spun down, sending up a bomb burst of water as it struck.

The pilot's parachute had opened all right. Richter circled him, watching as he inflated his bright yellow Mae West life-jacket. The Englishman seemed to be unhurt; he waved as his opponent flew low past him. There was plenty of British shipping in the area, and it would not be long before he was picked up.

Richter landed at St Pol twenty minutes later, his overheated engine groaning and shuddering. Two British fighters had been shot down, but three 109s were missing. It was clear that the Spitfire was going to be a formidable opponent.

The next morning, Fighter Wing 66 received new orders. The wing was to provide part of the escort for an all-out German bombing offensive against a single target: Dunkirk. Its aim was simple. To eliminate the British Expeditionary Force and the remnants of the French armies in the north, their backs against the sea.

*

Manston was like a beehive. There were aircraft everywhere, taking off or landing every couple of minutes or stacked around the circuit, waiting their turn. As well as Fighter Command's Spitfires and Hurricanes there were aircraft of Coastal Command too; Lockheed Hudsons and Avro Ansons, the latter made more warlike by the addition of machine-guns firing sideways through the fuselage windows. Antiquated Fairey Swordfish biplanes of the Fleet Air Arm, together with a flight of more modern Blackburn Skua dive-bombers, completed the motley picture.

The air battle over Dunkirk had flared up in earnest on 27 May, when wave after wave of Heinkels began pounding the port, the beaches and the armada of vessels offshore from first light onwards. Then the Stukas came, howling down over the shattered town, carpeting the harbour with their bombs. A French troopship was hit and capsized. Bodies floated in on the tide, forming a sodden khaki fringe along the beaches. Immediately after the Stukas came the Dorniers, droning over the town. From their elongated bellies sticks of bombs pirouetted down to explode among the inferno. Dunkirk's big oil storage tanks went up with a thud, sending a tremendous pillar of black smoke towering into the air.

Three hundred German bombers attacked Dunkirk that day, unloading 45,000 high-explosive and incendiary bombs into the ruins. The fires raged unabated; there had been no water supplies in the town for five days. By nightfall the harbour had been completely blocked, and the exhausted troops were compelled to mass on the beaches to await evacuation.

The RAF did what it could. Between dawn and dusk on 27 May, the sixteen fighter squadrons of No. 11 Group flew twenty-three patrols over Dunkirk and the beaches, destroying thirty-eight enemy aircraft for the loss of fourteen Spitfires and Hurricanes. Many more British fighters staggered back to base, however, with severe battle damage, and one squadron at Manston was so badly hit that it had to be moved north for a rest the following morning. 505 Squadron flew south to replace it, a move so rapid that the pilots had time to pack little more than their toothbrushes.

Yeoman's first patrol over Dunkirk was an experience he would never forget. Long before the French coast came in sight the pilots could see the vast cloud of smoke rising from the burning oil tanks, spreading like a dark banner across the sky. The acrid stench of it penetrated the cockpits, cloying the nostrils and making the eyes smart.

The Hurricanes skirted the smoke, flying at fifteen thousand feet along the stretch of coast between Gravelines and La Panne. Yeoman, looking down, was puzzled by dark shadows on the beaches, then he realized that the shadows were men — thousands of them, patiently awaiting their turn to be evacuated. Offshore, the Channel was packed with vessels of every shape and size; destroyers and minesweepers, ferries, fishing boats and small craft. At one point, he saw smoke rising from a large ship that lay burning and beached in the shallows.

For once, the Luftwaffe was absent from the sky. No enemy aircraft were sighted and the squadron turned for home. Shortly afterwards, a layer of low cloud crept across the sky, mingling with the smoke to form an impenetrable umbrella that afforded some protection at last to the battered men on the beaches. The cloud persisted all that day, and on the morning of the twenty-ninth fog and rain blanketed the Channel. Beneath the murk, unhindered by the Luftwaffe, the evacuation went ahead at a furious pace.

Then, early in the afternoon, the fog dispersed and the clouds began to break up. It was the signal for the holocaust to begin all over again. At three o'clock, no fewer than 180 Stukas hurled themselves on the harbour and the ships clustered around it, sinking several of them. Half an hour later it was the turn of twin-engined Junkers 88s, flying from newly captured bases in Holland.

The Hurricanes of 505 Squadron arrived right in the middle of this second attack, together with a squadron and a half of Spitfires. There was no time for preliminaries, for any fancy manoeuvring to get into a favourable position. The first wave of Junkers was already diving over the harbour and the British fighters went for them like terriers, every pilot selecting the target nearest to him. There were plenty of targets to choose from.

Yeoman saw a Junkers pulling out of its dive after releasing its bombs, and threw his fighter in pursuit. The 88 turned and headed inland, gaining speed. Yeoman lost it for a moment as it passed through a drifting smoke cloud, then picked it up again as it emerged from the other side. The German bomber was fast, but Yeoman closed the range and slowed it down with a three-second burst that set fire to its starboard engine. The 88 began to lose height, weaving gently from side to side. Yeoman fired again, and now thick black trails poured back from both the bomber's motors. Its dive became steeper and it went into the ground almost vertically, exploding in a great mushroom of smoke. Yeoman saw rivers of burning fuel spreading out like tentacles from the wreckage as he flew overhead.

He turned away and put the Hurricane into a climb, looking round to get his bearings. The fires of Dunkirk were ahead and to the left, some miles away. A lot of light flak started coming up at him, which meant that he had strayed over enemy territory. It was time to get out of it. He continued climbing, heading towards the coast.

He never heard the explosion of the cannon shell that hit the cockpit. He was conscious only of a vivid flash, temporarily blinding him, and of a stinging pain as a shell splinter sliced across his forehead. A howling gale entered the cockpit as the canopy disintegrated. Dimly he heard a series of rapid bangs, coming from somewhere behind him, and the rattle of more splinters against the armour-plate of his seat back.

The stick banged uselessly against his knee. He looked around, raising a hand to wipe away the blood that streamed into his eyes. The Hurricane's tail had gone. There was no sign of his attacker.

Frantically, he unfastened his seat harness and reached up to pull back what was left of the cockpit hood. It refused to budge. He tried again, bracing his feet against the instrument panel. The slipstream shrieked about his ears as the Hurricane plummeted down. He threw himself against the side of the cockpit in panic. A screaming voice sounded in his ears, as though from a long way off. He failed to recognize it as his own.

A face rose in front of him, sharp against the blurred earth. Julia. Oh God, he cried, let me live.

He gave a last, despairing heave and the hood came free at last, jerking back on its runners. Sobbing with relief, he heaved himself out of his seat and flung himself head-first over the side. The cushion of the airflow carried him over the trailing edge of the wing, plucking him clear of the doomed fighter.

Later, he could not recall having pulled the D-ring. All he remembered was the sudden crack of his parachute opening, the blissful swaying as he drifted down.

Suddenly, his stomach twisted in apprehension as he realized that he might still be over enemy-held territory. He looked down. He was drifting over a maze of canals and waterways, intersected by an occasional road. Hamlets were dotted here and there, some of them in flames.

He still had no idea what had shot him down. The sky was empty. As he floated down, he became aware of other sounds above the whisper of the wind in his parachute lines; a kind of popping noise, like the crackle of twigs on a fire, and sporadic dull thuds. It looked as though he was going to land right in the middle of a pitched battle.

He hit the ground heavily, beside a small clump of trees, and his parachute dragged him along the ground for several yards before he managed to release himself. Breathing heavily, he sat up. He saw movement ahead of him, and reached down to pull his revolver from his flying boot. It wasn't there. It must have fallen out during his exit from the Hurricane.

Three or four soldiers came doubling towards him, crouching low and running forward in short bursts. Their field-grey uniforms and coal-scuttle helmets left Yeoman in no doubt about their identity. Wildly, he looked round, wondering if he could reach the copse before they caught up with him. In that same instant, he knew he couldn't make it. He had hurt his ankle slightly on landing and he would not be able to move fast enough. In any case, the Germans were close enough to cut him down easily.

He stood up painfully and raised his hands. He felt no emotion. The only thought in his mind was that it might be worse. Suddenly, all he wanted was to lie down and go to sleep.

The leading German doubled up and crumpled forward as though in slow motion, clasping his stomach. The others fell sideways, like a row of skittles. Yeoman swung round, startled, the burst of gunfire ringing in his ears. A man in khaki crouched by the edge of the copse, a smoking Bren light machine-gun slung from his shoulder at the hip-firing position. He waved urgently at the pilot. Yeoman felt a great surge of relief and stumbled towards him, wincing with the pain of his ankle. The man, a corporal, grabbed him by the arm and urged him into the shelter of the trees.

'You're lucky, mate,' the soldier said. 'Another twenty minutes and we wouldn't be here anymore. We're the rearguard, and we've orders to fall back behind the Bergues Canal on the Dunkirk perimeter. That was a Jerry recce patrol I just clobbered; their pals won't be far behind.'

Yeoman saw that the copse was full of soldiers. He learned that they were men of the 4th Battalion, the South Durham Regiment. They were just about on their last legs; most of them had had no real sleep for three weeks, having been involved in continuous fighting all the way back from the river Dyle. The corporal grinned at Yeoman through a layer of grime and stubble.

'We saw you get the Jerry,' he said. 'The lads here gave you a bit of a cheer. We thought you'd had it, though, when you got hit.'

'What shot me down?' Yeoman wanted to know, out of curiosity.

The corporal shrugged. 'We never saw any Jerry fighters,' he said, 'so I reckon it must have been ack-ack. They have some light stuff, which they move up with their forward units.'

A lieutenant came running up through the trees and held a short conversation with the corporal. The officer turned to Yeoman. 'All right,' he said, 'you'd better move back with "A" Company. You'll find them on the other side of the wood. Don't waste any time — Jerry will be bringing up his mortars in a minute to give this place a pasting.'

Yeoman limped off and found 'A' Company without difficulty, reporting to its commander, a young captain whose left hand was wrapped in a blood-soaked bandage. Ten minutes later the company set off in good order along a narrow road that bordered one of the area's many canals, trudging wearily towards the fires of Dunkirk. On the other side of the road, the fields were littered with burning vehicles. Some had been left half on the road, and their heat scorched the men as they trooped past.

As they marched on, a drum-roll of explosions echoed behind them. Yeoman paused and looked back. Over the copse they had just left, yellowish smoke was rising as the Germans carpeted the area with mortar shells. The crackle of rifle and machine-gun fire drifted on the breeze. After a while, there was silence.

*

Joachim Richter crouched among the sand dunes, feeling utterly dejected. He looked at the dirty, unshaven men around him, clad in their stained and tattered khaki, and shuddered inwardly. It would not require much of an excuse, he thought, for one of them to put a bullet through him.

He still didn't know fully what had happened. It had been an uneventful patrol over the Dunkirk sector, with no enemy fighters to be seen, the Messerschmitts skirting the British and French anti-aircraft defences around the port. Suddenly there had been a massive jolt and his Emil had gone out of control. Someone must have collided with him; probably that idiot Schöner, who couldn't hold station properly if his life depended on it. Anyway, Richter had baled out in the nick of time and had landed just inside the northern sector of the Dunkirk perimeter, where some French troops had taken him prisoner. They had been all for shooting him on the spot, but some British soldiers had arrived just in time to save his skin.

For the past twenty-four hours he had cowered miserably among the dunes, discovering what it was like to be on the receiving end of his own side's bombs and shells. A shallow fox-hole, scooped out of the sand, seemed pitiful protection against the machine-gun bullets of the Messerschmitts that dived down frequently to strafe the beaches. For Joachim Richter, life just at the moment seemed pretty bleak; a choice between being killed by his own people, or if he survived, a prison camp somewhere in England.

He looked up, past his captors, as yet another line of soldiers filed down on to the beach to await evacuation. Because of the incessant Luftwaffe attacks, troops were now being taken off only after dark.

With sudden interest, Richter noticed a blue uniform among the khaki. So this, he thought, is what one of his RAF opponents looked like at close quarters. The man saw him at the same instant and wandered over, curiosity on his face.

So it came about that, on a bullet-swept, bomb-torn beach two miles west of Braye Dunes, two young men who had already met more than once in air combat, but would never know it, at last stood face to face through one of the incredible coincidences that occur so often in time of war.

Richter had learned some English at school. He had never been very good at it, but he recalled enough to make himself understood. He got up, carefully brushing the sand from his uniform, and nodded coolly at the Englishman.

'Richter,' he said, 'Leutnant, Reichsluftwaffe. Good afternoon.'

Yeoman nodded back. 'Oh, really,' he said, determined not to be dragged into a tea-party conversation. Richter stiffened slightly, his English sufficient to comprehend the other's slight insult.

'I will not be a prisoner for long,' he continued. 'Soon, the German Army will invade England.'

'Balls,' Yeoman said, and turned away. Strangely enough, he felt no antagonism towards the young pilot. Richter's presence on the beach, and his subsequent fate, was a matter of complete indifference to him.

Yeoman walked back to where the South Durhams were waiting, sprawled on the sand in small groups. Someone produced a looted tin of damsons and, miracle of miracles, some bully beef. A soldier handed a few morsels of the food to the pilot and he wolfed them down, conscious of the fact that he had eaten nothing since five o'clock that morning. Then, all at once, he felt guilty as the realization came to him that the exhausted men around him had probably eaten nothing for days.

Suddenly they were all burrowing into the sand like moles as a cluster of shells, hurled by heavy German guns far inland, erupted across the beach. The barrage went on for ten minutes, the explosions lifting great geysers of sand and debris — human as well as material — into the air. Then the shellfire crept out to sea, searching out the ships and boats in the Channel. The silence after the barrage seemed unearthly, broken only by the occasional cry of a wounded man or the broken sobbing of those whose nerve had gone. Yeoman spat out sand; his head ached intolerably and there was a stabbing pain in his ears. Blood trickled from the cut on his forehead; the dressing placed over it by one of the soldiers had come undone. He staunched the flow as best he could.

There was to be little respite. After the shelling came the dive-bombers, sweeping over Dunkirk from the south-east. They spread out, some going for the town, others for the beaches and still others for the ships. Two of them, having unloaded their bombs, raced low over the beach almost wingtip to wingtip, blazing away with their front guns. Yeoman, sickened, saw a group of soldiers run to find better cover, only to be cut down like com under a reaper.

Then, above the snarl of the Stukas' engines, a new sound intervened: a sound that Yeoman knew too well; the scream of Rolls-Royce Merlins under full power. He risked a glance skywards, just in time to see a dozen Hurricanes hurl themselves on the dive-bombers. The latter's Messerschmitt escort came tumbling like an avalanche from their vantage point, several thousand feet higher up, and a whirling dogfight developed over the beaches.

Yeoman saw one Hurricane pursuing a fleeing Stuka over the sea, flying along the line of the beach so low that the dive-bomber's undercarriage almost touched the water. He saw the Stuka explode, its burning debris falling into the sea, and the victorious Hurricane weave away through a cloud of shellbursts, its pilot doubtless cursing naval gunners whose aircraft recognition was not of the best.

His attention was captured by the sound of tortured engines above his head. He looked up and saw a Hurricane and a 109 turning round and round, chasing each other's tail and striving to gain the advantage. At last, as though by mutual agreement, they both rolled out of the turn and charged head-on at each other, firing with everything they had. Yeoman dug his fingernails into his palms as they raced towards what appeared to be certain destruction. Then, just when a collision seemed inevitable, the Messerschmitt pulled up sharply. The Hurricane's last burst of fire slammed into its vulnerable belly, where the fuel tank was situated, and the German fighter instantly became a fireball, falling like a comet towards the ruins of Dunkirk.

The Hurricane had been mortally hit, too. It went into a dive, trailing a ribbon of smoke that quickly became thicker and shot with flame. Yeoman cheered inwardly as the dark shape of the pilot detached itself, falling for long, agonizing seconds before its parachute opened and brought it drifting steadily towards Yeoman's bit of beach.

The next moment, the young pilot was running frantically through the sand, screaming at the top of his voice to a group of soldiers who had raised their rifles and were firing rapidly at the man dangling helplessly beneath the parachute.

'Bastards,' he screamed. 'Stupid bastards! He's one of ours!'

It was too late. The figure under the parachute jerked several times, then hung limply. It hit the dunes in a flurry of sand and the parachute floated over it like a shroud.

Yeoman reached the spot, gasping for breath, and barged through the men who had converged on the collapsed parachute and its burden. Some were weeping unashamedly. No one could blame them for their mistake; they had seen so few Allied aircraft during the past weeks that everything in the sky had come to be classed as enemy.

He threw himself on his knees by the side of the motionless pilot. The man lay on his back, blood soaking into the sand around him. His eyes were wide open and he was dead.

It was Flight-Lieutenant Rogerson.

# CHAPTER TWELVE

They went down to the water's edge after dark, to embark in the armada of small craft that closed in to take them to the larger vessels that were hove to in deeper water. Yeoman shuffled forward with the rest, part of a long, dark snake of men who were so tired that they would probably have marched into the water until it closed over their heads, had someone ordered them to. Away to their left, the fires of Dunkirk formed a great glow in the darkness, punctuated by the more vivid flashes of exploding bombs and shells.

The queue Yeoman had joined moved slowly out along an improvised jetty made of army lorries, standing nose to tail in the shallows. Apart from the rumble of explosions to the rear, the period of waiting passed relatively quietly. Yeoman was troubled badly by thirst, but no one had anything to drink.

After four hours, the group he was with reached the head of the queue. Quietly, without any fuss, the weary soldiers and the pilot clambered into one of the naval whalers that were providing a ferry service to the waiting ships. Yeoman squashed in near the stem; the craft was laden to the gunwales and salt water slopped over his legs as the ratings who manned her pulled away from the shore.

The drone of engines overhead lent impetus to their efforts. They had almost reached their goal, a freighter that loomed like a great wall ahead of them in the darkness, when the first flares cascaded down.

'Oh, Christ,' someone said quietly. 'Now we're for it.'

In the brutal light of the flares, impressions stamped themselves vividly on Yeoman's mind. The great bulk of the ship, the glittering sea, and above all, the white and terrified faces of the men. Among them, one in particular stood out; that of the German, Richter, crouching at the opposite end of the boat.

A stick of bombs wailed down, the noise of their fall swelling until it blotted out everything else. A great concussion slammed at them, and Yeoman's world turned upside down.

He was choking, drowning in oily water. He struck out blindly, searching for something, anything, that would help him to cling to life. A wave lifted him and hurled him brutally against something solid, hard and cold. The hull of a ship. Half stunned, he floundered along it and his groping fingers closed around a rope net. He clung desperately to it, fighting the rise and fall of the ship and the battering of the sea.

Someone was slipping a rope under his armpits, prising his fingers loose from their iron grasp on the ropes. 'Come on, matey,' a voice cried in his ear, 'it's all right now.' His body bumped painfully against the side of the ship and then he was collapsing over the rail, a sodden bundle, retching up sea water. Someone threw a blanket round his shoulders and he sat on a coil of rope, shivering. Sometime later, the deck beneath him vibrated to the steady rhythm of the ship's engines as she got under way, nosing out into the darkened Channel with her exhausted human cargo.

\*

The German soldiers moved slowly to the water's edge, picking their way past the piles of abandoned equipment and the groups of Allied prisoners who clustered on the beach, under guard.

One soldier, an engineer, looked with interest at a wooden jetty built by the British during the early stage of the evacuation. It had withstood a great deal of pounding.

Well, he thought, no one would be using it now. It was the morning of 3 June, and most of the beaches were in enemy hands. Only a small pocket of the enemy, mostly French, still held the shrunken perimeter in Dunkirk itself, and they would not last for much longer.

The engineer went forward until the waves lapped his boots. Suddenly he leaned forward, peering at a dark shape that lay half in and half out of the water underneath the jetty.

It was a man, his arms locked around one of the wooden posts. The engineer waded in for a closer look, and his mouth dropped open in amazement when he saw the insignia of a Luftwaffe officer.

He shouted for help, and with the aid of a couple of soldiers managed to release the man and drag him out of the water. They laid him down on the sand and looked at one another.

'He must have been shot down and taken prisoner,' the engineer said, 'then got away and hidden under the jetty. God knows how long he'd been clinging on like that, with the Tommies tramping over his head. Days, probably.'

One of the other soldiers nodded. 'Well,' he said, 'he's a goner now, that's for sure.'

The engineer, on an impulse, knelt beside the inert figure and placed his hand on the Luftwaffe officer's left breast, underneath the drenched tunic.

Startled, he looked up at the others.

Then he jumped to his feet and ran up the beach, shouting loudly for a stretcher.

Printed in Poland
by Amazon Fulfillment
Poland Sp. z o.o., Wrocław